THE HATCHARDS
CRIME
COMPANION

THE HATCHARDS CRIME COMPANION

100 Top Crime Novels
Selected by the Crime Writers' Association

Edited by
SUSAN MOODY

A 'Hatchards 100 Series' Publication

First published in Great Britain in 1990
by Hatchards, 187 Piccadilly, London W1V 9DA

British Library Cataloguing in Publishing Data
Hatchard's crime companion : the top 100 crime novels of all time. –
(100 series).
1. Crime fiction in English – Bibliographies
I. Title II. Moody, Susan
016.8230872

ISBN 0–904030–02–4

All title information contained in this book was correct at the time of
going to press. However the price and continued availability of books
are subject to alteration at the publishers' discretion.

Designed by Roger Lightfoot
Typeset by Selectmove
Made and Printed in Great Britain
by Cox and Wyman Ltd, Reading

Contents

Section Three – The Critics   121

Section Four – The Crime Writers' Association   133

Foreword

LEN DEIGHTON

Anyone with time and leisure enough to create the world's most perfect club would probably start with the site. London is the only place for a club. New York clubs are stuffy and Dublin clubs too quiet. Los Angeles clubs are not clubs at all, just expensive restaurants. The perfect club would have to be in the West End of London, in Piccadilly or St. James. It would have an old-fashioned exterior and a door that jammed in the wet weather. It would have some battered old sofas (not those back-breaking leather-buttoned chesterfields) and an unending supply of tea and coffee. Add a cosy atmosphere, lots of odd staircases in unexpected places, and nooks and corners that even the oldest member has not fully explored. It would also have to have something that clubs – especially English clubs – do not normally excel in: a welcome for old friends and for strangers too. Members would have to be reserved but genial; staff learned and shrewd but not judgemental. No muzak. No regimental doormen.

But unless the members were going to stand around looking at each other all day, it would have to have books. I don't mean a book here and there or those dusty old volumes that decorate the walls of many London clubs. I mean real books. Shelves filled with books; walls filled with books. Books up the staircases and piled up on the floor. Books in cupboards and books in the sink. Rare books and popular books, expensive illustrated books and cheap paperback books. I'd want it to have books on antiques, architecture, sports and games. Books on health and on economics and aviation. Old books and new books. Books on current affairs while the affairs are still current. Books on science and football and crustaceans and cookery. Calligraphy and graphology; astrology and astronomy. Reverent memoirs and revealing biography. Atlases and Bibles; classics and poetry and books on the theatre and film and photography and perhaps, here and there, some fiction too.

Members would be able to buy any book that they wanted to take home. And do it by means of a signature. And pay later. This would mean being tempted very much and very often. So I would insist that my club charged no subscription. Members would be able to go in and out of my club without signing a visitors' book. They'd find it a convenient place to meet their friends and indulge in gossip. Country members might want to have a meeting place outside London – for instance Ipswich, Tunbridge Wells or even Watford.

There is a place like this in Piccadilly, London. It's been there since 1797 and it's called Hatchards. But we must all put the pressure on if we are ever to get those soft sofas and the tea and coffee.

Now our club has decided to publish a series of books that will appeal to book maniacs like me. In association with all my old and dear friends in the Crime Writers' Association, Hatchards have taken the big step of producing their first book. It is a delightful, informative and amusing book about crime fiction. It is not written only for crime buffs, it is for people who like to know what is voted top. Naturally I am extremely flattered to find myself in the 'most wanted list' and wedged between Chandler and Hammett with Wilkie Collins for company.

For Harry Keating in his splendid piece on the great man (see page 58) tells us:

> 'Wilkie Collins, sitting up there on his comfortably puffy cloud, his two simultaneous mistresses and their families happily grouped on clouds to either side . . .'

Yes, well, I thought it was a bit crowded up here. But what conversation! For those who want to wonder if the crime story is a crime novel – or if the crime novel is art – there is plenty here to fuel argument. Here are some writers who some might not think of in connection with the crime novel: Graham Greene and John Fowles rub shoulders with Ian and Agatha. There is something for everyone. Is there a reader with a soul so dead that he can read *A Kiss Before Dying* without nodding respectfully to the author? On page 80 Lesley Grant-Adamson – reading it for this book – says it 'shot into my personal top ten'. So it will for many who come to it for the first time. So will lots of other recommendations from this compendious work.

Here the 'whodunnits' are distinguished from the 'psychological' and the 'hardboiled' from the 'thrillers'. Here are words of wisdom and words of caution. Favourite writers such as Julian Symons, Harry Keating and Tim Heald in their years of reviewing must have read more books than were good for them. Their opinions – like those of all the contributors – are valuable to old-timers and tyros: readers and writers and booksellers too. All will know, in the words of John Wainwright on page 70, 'The art is not so simple anymore'.

This book is a wonderful idea carried through with the care and attention that I have come to expect from Hatchards and from the widely-read and dedicated professionals of the CWA. What a good job they have done in reminding us of superlative writing to go back to, and alerting us to the joys of outstanding works we might have missed. What dull fellow would get half-way through this book without scribbling a 'wants' list? And what imperturbable personality could get to the end of this book without one cry of rage?

Is there no bad word to say? Yes, there is. This kind of selection process must always depend more upon fame than talent. Remember that it is a vote for single books, and sometimes for the one-book author. Such selections will always favour the old and venerable while the new and exciting get out-voted. (Someone might care to calculate the average age of the top 50.) And a disturbing percentage of the chosen books are surely remembered for the films made from them. Writers are a conservative bunch and, as you will see, they go for the established 'classics'.

As a way of discovering and rediscovering old loves this book has no equal, but next time you are browsing in our favourite club don't forget the first books of young talented writers who need you as readers.

Introduction

SUSAN MOODY

Trying to categorise crime fiction is like trying to pack a water bed into a suitcase. However hard you try, there are always going to be bits that can't be fitted in. Is *Rogue Male* a novel of suspense or an action thriller? Does *The Daughter of Time* really count as a history mystery? Can spy fiction be classed along with crime? And so on.

When we first circulated the membership of the Crime Writers' Association with a questionnaire asking people to name their favourite writers in various categories, we discovered that it was necessary to be fairly arbitrary about the choice of those categories, so wide is the spectrum covered by the blanket title of Crime Fiction. No, we said: we won't sub-divide Police Procedural into the British and the American variety but we *would* include a Hardboiled category. Yes, we agreed: Espionage should be included, so should Romantic Suspense, despite those purists who jib at the former and positively sneer at the latter, on the grounds that they aren't true crime fiction. We believe they are, and those writing about them in the body of this book argue ably for their inclusion.

How, you may wonder, did this book come to be embarked upon in the first place? It began with a party, as so many of the best ideas do, and went on from there to surface in the Marketing Department of

Hatchards where Andrew Holgate, having examined it from all angles, decided it was an idea worth pursuing. He got in touch with me, suggesting that it might be rather fun to produce a list of books chosen by the CWA for the benefit of his customers. The idea was put to the CWA and greeted enthusiastically, for three main reasons. Firstly, it gave us an opportunity to see which authors of crime fiction had engaged the attention of their peers in the past and were doing so now. Secondly, we thought it might generate some excitement, even some debate. Thirdly, because, as far as we could ascertain, it had never been done before.

Over the years there have been several attempts to draw up a definitive list of the top crime novels ever written, but these have always been the choice of one expert or, in one American case, the choice of readers. The books chosen herein have been selected by the workers at the coal-face themselves: the people who actually write the books.

It should be emphasised that the contributors were asked to name their *favourite* books, not necessarily those they considered the best. Categories were used simply because it was felt that to ask the CWA to name their favourite fifty books without further subdivision would be asking for trouble – and could lead to no reponse at all. Instead, we were sneaky: all we asked was that they name five books in each of ten categories. Some, of course, unable to let a favourite author be passed over, named many more than five. The problem with such a method of choosing books was that many of the more prolific authors received a wide range of votes without any significant weighting towards a single title: we have therefore included a list of authors to indicate this (see page 53).

The use of the word 'favourite' may well account for

the number of books chosen which date from the Fifties and earlier and almost certainly reflects to a certain extent the excitement we all felt on discovering crime fiction for the first time, back in our collective youths. But there are plenty of recent names on the list as well, which should be an added interest both for new readers of the genre, and for those with already-established favourites of their own.

Everybody enjoys making lists, though some found the task of choosing a mere fifty out of the vast and diverse range of good crime fiction currently available was beyond them. Most people, however, agreed that the exercise was both interesting and stimulating. The crime genre itself is obviously not only alive and well but developing all the time.

For the purposes of producing these lists, I have had to read a number of crime novels which might otherwise have escaped my attention. In some cases it was also helpful to see what the experts thought; there are two books in particular on the novel of crime and detection which no crime buff should be without. One of these is Julian Symons' comprehensive survey of the genre, *Bloody Murder*, which first appeared in 1972 and was extensively revised in 1985. The other is Melvyn Barnes' guide to two centuries of crime fiction, entitled *Murder In Print*, published by Barn Owl Books in 1986.

Most of those who completed the questionnaire said how much fun it had been – and how difficult. There was a considerable amount of agonising over old favourites which had to be passed over in favour of new ones. It's like choosing eight records for *Desert Island Discs*: how can you possibly be expected to reduce the entire range of favourite listening down to just eight? In the same way, how can you pick, out of a lifetime of reading, just five suspense novels, five whodunnits, five police procedurals and so on? What proved interesting was that in each of the ten categories, the top favourite was so far ahead of the rest of the field.

Some people worried about where to place their choices. Does *Gaudy Night* count as Golden Age or as Romantic Suspense – or even as a straight Whodunnit? Is *The False Inspector Dew* a Whodunnit or a History Mystery? Romantic Suspense and Police Procedurals, you might think, speak for themselves, but where does Psychological Suspense fit in? And the Golden Age: where does that start – or end? (For our purposes we proposed that it began in 1914 and ended in 1939). And what about Hardboiled?

Yes: what *about* Hardboiled? Nobody seemed to have much trouble in slotting Chandler in there, Hammett, too. So much so that the Hardboiled list ends up being somewhat repetitious and there are four Chandler novels included in the first fifty on the list. It might have been expected that the Top Ten in each category would have made up the list of One Hundred, but in fact this turned out not to be so. For instance, more votes might be given to No. 9 on the Whodunnit list than to No. 6 on the Romantic Suspense.

It might be worth mentioning that the writers of crime novels are not necessarily readers of them as well. And of those who are, there are many who stick firmly to just a few categories: some never read action thrillers, others loathe police procedurals – and very few men read Romantic Suspense.

In order to examine the various categories in greater detail, we have asked ten practitioners in different sub-genres to write about them. No parameters were laid down, no editorial line insisted on. The essays make interesting reading. Similarly, we asked four well-known critics to tell us what they look for (or hope not to find) when they open a new batch of novels for reviewing. Idiosyncratic views of the genre can only open it up for further debate – and perhaps encourage the purchasing of books that might otherwise not have been read.

Looking at the lists, do they indicate any new directions in crime writing? Certainly the fact that a list of twenty female detectives can be drawn up is indicative of one of the more interesting trends in the past decade or so: the rise of the woman protagonist. And these are not the Miss van Snoops and Rosika Storeys of former years, nor even the Miss Marples and Dame Beatrice Bradleys, all of them independent, intuitive and inventive – until it comes to tidying up the loose ends, at which point a MAN is inevitably brought in, be it nephew, lover, friend or colleague.

But that has changed in the last decade. Sara Paretsky's V.I. Warshawski is perhaps tougher than most, a truly hardboiled female, but there are plenty of others. And this illustrates crime fiction's most abiding strength: the fact that it mirrors social changes at a far greater speed than mainstream literature. It has to. The crime novel relies for its impact upon its immediacy and its relevance to life outside the pages, and one of the most significant social changes in the past fifty years must surely be the status of women. So these days, writers are producing female protagonists who are real women. They endure heart-break or the Inland Revenue man, they fight prejudice and loneliness, as well as villains, they worry about walking down the mean streets; they are not invincible, any more than their true-life counterparts are. Quite often they drink hard liquor. Sometimes they get into bed with a man who is – gasp! – not their husband and whom, what's more, they have no intention of marrying. On top of all that, they solve the crimes in which they find themselves involved without male help.

If I were to make any predictions – and no one looks more of an idiot than the prophet ten years on – I would say there will be fewer hardboiled novels in the years to come. As the age grows more violent about us, and Armageddon is predicted for 1999, the hardboiled guy seems to me to have outgrown his society. The New Man may be something of a myth, but that does not mean that the Marlowes and Spades of the 1990s really exist. Despite everything, we are, I believe, a more personally compassionate society – and toughness is out of fashion.

The tumbling of the walls surrounding Eastern Bloc countries excited some speculation among writers of espionage fiction. With no more Berlin Wall to be crossed, was the spy novel finished? Of course not. Spying is the second oldest profession, after all, and where there are two countries there will always be at least four spies: one on each side and two who are double agents. Where there are spies there are stories and with Northern Ireland set to run and run, with the Middle Eastern countries flexing their political muscles, with the troubles in Central America and the cracking edifice of Russian hegemony, the espionage writer will never be short of material.

Another trend may well be the increase in romantic suspense. Evelyn Anthony and Mary Stewart have ably led the field for years but by now their successors must be somewhere in the pipeline. The big crime novels, too, such as *Presumed Innocent* (by Scott Turow) or *The Silence of the Lambs* (by Thomas Harris) still seem to be mainly an American phenomenon, but will certainly emerge over here very shortly.

Meanwhile, I expect the Great British Crime Novel in all its forms to sweep triumphantly through the next decade and on into the 21st century, gathering accolades all the way, and changing, as it has since the beginning, to reflect changing times and mores.

Susan Moody entered the field of crime fiction in 1984 with a book featuring Penny Wanawake, her series heroine, who is a tall black photographer as well as a reluctant amateur sleuth. She has since written six more Penny novels and a mystery thriller called Playing With Fire *(published by Macdonald). She was Chairman of the CWA between 1988 and 1990 and is on the Executive Committee of the International Association of Crime Writers.*

The Lists

The hundred favourite crime novels, as chosen by the crime writers themselves, with discussion and commentary. All opinions are the editor's except where otherwise stated; the edition quoted for each entry is the current paperback one, except where only a hardback edition exists. Subsidiary lists include favourite writers and detectives, both male and female, and even one who is a little bit of both – or possibly neither.

1. THE DAUGHTER OF TIME
Josephine Tey (1951)

2. THE BIG SLEEP
Raymond Chandler (1939)

3. THE SPY WHO CAME IN FROM THE COLD
John le Carré (1963)

4. GAUDY NIGHT
Dorothy L. Sayers (1935)

5. THE MURDER OF ROGER ACKROYD
Agatha Christie (1926)

6. REBECCA
Daphne du Maurier (1938)

7. FAREWELL MY LOVELY
Raymond Chandler (1940)

8. THE MOONSTONE
Wilkie Collins (1868)

9. THE IPCRESS FILE
Len Deighton (1962)

10. THE MALTESE FALCON
Dashiell Hammett (1930)

11. THE FRANCHISE AFFAIR
Josephine Tey (1948)

12. LAST SEEN WEARING
Hillary Waugh (1952)

13. THE NAME OF THE ROSE
Umberto Eco (1980)

14. ROGUE MALE
Geoffrey Household (1939)

15. THE LONG GOODBYE
Raymond Chandler (1953)

16. MALICE AFORETHOUGHT
Francis Iles (1931)

17. THE DAY OF THE JACKAL
Frederick Forsyth (1971)

18. THE NINE TAILORS
Dorothy L. Sayers (1934)

38. STRANGERS ON A TRAIN
Patricia Highsmith (1950)

39. JUDGEMENT IN STONE
Ruth Rendell (1977)

40. THE HOLLOW MAN
John Dickson Carr (1938)

41. THE POISONED CHOCOLATES CASE
Anthony Berkeley (1929)

42.= A MORBID TASTE FOR BONES
Ellis Peters (1977)

42.= THE LEPER OF ST. GILES
Ellis Peters (1981)

44. A KISS BEFORE DYING
Ira Levin (1953)

45. THE TALENTED MR. RIPLEY
Patricia Highsmith (1955)

46. BRIGHTON ROCK
Graham Greene (1938)

47. THE LADY IN THE LAKE
Raymond Chandler (1943)

48. PRESUMED INNOCENT
Scott Turow (1987)

49. A DEMON IN MY VIEW
Ruth Rendell (1976)

50.= THE DEVIL IN VELVET
John Dickson Carr (1951)

50.= A FATAL INVERSION
Barbara Vine (1987)

52. THE JOURNEYING BOY
Michael Innes (1949)

53. A TASTE FOR DEATH
P.D. James (1986)

54. THE EAGLE HAS LANDED
Jack Higgins (1975)

55. MY BROTHER MICHAEL
Mary Stewart (1960)

56.= BERTIE AND THE TIN MAN
Peter Lovesey (1987)

56.= PENNY BLACK
Susan Moody (1984)

80. THE KILLINGS AT
BADGER'S DRIFT
Caroline Graham (1987)

81.= THE BEAST MUST
DIE
Nicholas Blake (1938)

81.= GORKY PARK
Martin Cruz Smith (1981)

83. DEATH COMES AS THE
END
Agatha Christie (1945)

84. GREEN FOR DANGER
Christianna Brand (1945)

85. TRAGEDY AT LAW
Cyril Hare (1942)

86. THE COLLECTOR
John Fowles (1963)

87. GIDEON'S DAY
J.J. Marric (1955)

88. THE SUN CHEMIST
Lionel Davidson (1976)

89. THE GUNS OF
NAVARONE
Alistair Maclean (1957)

90. THE COLOUR OF
MURDER
Julian Symons (1957)

91. GREENMANTLE
John Buchan (1916)

92. THE RIDDLE OF THE
SANDS
Erskine Childers (1903)

93. WOBBLE TO DEATH
Peter Lovesey (1970)

94. RED HARVEST
Dashiell Hammett (1929)

95. THE KEY TO
REBECCA
Ken Follett (1980)

96. SADIE WHEN SHE
DIED
Ed McBain (1972)

97. THE MURDER OF THE
MAHARAJAH
H.R.F. Keating (1980)

98. WHAT BLOODY MAN
IS THAT?
Simon Brett (1987)

99. SHOOTING SCRIPT
Gavin Lyall (1966)

100. FOUR JUST MEN
Edgar Wallace (1906)

1. THE DAUGHTER OF TIME   *Josephine Tey*

1951   191 pages, Penguin, £3.99 paperback

Tey's hero, Inspector Alan Grant, hospitalised after a fall, relieves the tedium by attempting to solve the mystery of who really murdered the Princes in the Tower. Was Richard III the subject of a smear campaign or did Shakespeare get it right? With the help of a young American who follows up the various lines of historical research suggested by Grant, he comes to a conclusion which, though not startlingly original, nonetheless makes the reader feel closely involved in the unravelling of a complicated plot. The theme has been brought up to date in *The Wench Is Dead*, Colin Dexter's CWA Gold Dagger-winning story, in which a bedridden Inspector Morse takes apart a murder case from the 1800s and puts it together again with a solution which differs from the official verdict at the time.

2. THE BIG SLEEP   *Raymond Chandler*

1939   220 pages, Penguin, £4.50 paperback

The first of Raymond Chandler's seven crime novels, all of which are classic examples of the Hardboiled School which he perfected. His pre-eminence in the genre is amply demonstrated by the fact that he has four novels in the top fifty, each of which exemplifies the author's perceptive eye for character and ambience, and demonstrates his keen ear for wisecracking dialogue and social observation. In each, Philip Marlowe fulminates against corruption in high places and the indifference the Haves display to the plight of the Have-Nots. Here, wheelchair-bound General Sternwood invites Marlowe to deal with gambling debts run up by his dissolute daughter, Carmen, and so launches him into a world of blackmail, murder and high stakes.

3. THE SPY WHO CAME IN FROM THE COLD
John le Carré

1963
220 pages, Coronet, £3.50 paperback

The book which finally thrust the realities of the Great Game into bleak perspective, showing definitively that Our Lot is no better – but no worse – than the Other Side. Soaked in a doom-laden sense of expedient betrayal and cynical deceit, this is the one which took the heroics out of spying once and for all.

4. GAUDY NIGHT *Dorothy L. Sayers*

1935   446 pages, Coronet, £3.99 paperback

A classic crime story memorable for the lack of blood and bodies. Crime writer Harriet Vane finds herself caught up in a spate of poison-pen letters which have been plaguing the female dons of her old Oxford college. Asked to solve the case, she is unable to make much headway and calls upon the aristocratic talents of Lord Peter Wimsey, who was responsible for her own acquittal on a murder charge in Sayers' earlier book, *Strong Poison (see No. 67)*. Not a popular book with critics, partly because of the author's somewhat naive claim that in writing it she had transcended the pure novel of detection and moved into the realms of intellectual integrity. However, it remains beloved by readers.

5. THE MURDER OF ROGER ACKROYD
   Agatha Christie

1926   235 pages, Fontana, £3.25 paperback

Christie's *tour de force*: although it features Hercule Poirot, it breaks away entirely from the conventions of detective story writing as they existed in the 1920s and became the turning point in her career. It would not be playing fair to give away the plot; suffice it to say that despite accusations of cheating, every clue is scrupulously placed in front of the reader. Who *did* murder Roger Ackroyd? If you've never done so, read it and find out.

6. REBECCA   *Daphne du Maurier*

1938   397 pages, Pan, £3.99 paperback

Every second wife's nightmare, this is the story of a diffident young woman whose marriage is overshadowed by the image of her husband's brilliant and beautiful first wife, the Rebecca of the title. Du Maurier's ability to complicate a plot with unspoken misconceptions, while never once letting up on the tension, is shown at its very best in this deservedly successful novel of romantic suspense.

7. FAREWELL MY LOVELY   *Raymond Chandler*

1940   254 pages, Penguin, £4.50 paperback

Moose Malloy – 'a big man but no more than six foot five inches tall and not wider than a beer truck' – is out of the pen after 8 years and looking for his sweetheart Velma. Out of curiosity, PI Philip Marlowe tags along, and finds himself drugged, sapped and shot at for his troubles. The result is classic Chandler, which more than compensates for the slightly caricatured portrait of Malloy with a mazy plot and fine, controlled writing. (*Andrew Holgate*)

8. THE MOONSTONE   *Wilkie Collins*

1868   528 pages, Penguin, £2.99 paperback

The first, the longest and the best of detective novels, according to T. S. Eliot, who clearly didn't rate *Crime and Punishment (1866)*, this is puzzle-devising of the most ingenious kind grafted onto a gripping plot. It became the model for hundreds of subsequent crime novels and contains all the classical elements you could wish for: drug abuse, murder, suicide, a missing diamond, sinister foreigners and a multi-viewpoint method of story-telling which keeps the action swinging along. It is remarkable, too, for the portrait Collins provides of a policeman who is no mere PC Plod but a man with sharply-drawn personal quirks, again a model for the future.

9. THE IPCRESS FILE   *Len Deighton*

1962   272 pages, Grafton, £2.95 paperback

In which the unnamed working-class hero strips the 007 gloss off the business of modern spying and shows its dark and immoral underbelly. Together with John le Carré (whose spy came in from the cold the following year), Deighton manages to write with ironic humour about the day-to-day routine of official betrayal, while at the same time exploring the heartless ethics involved.

10. THE MALTESE FALCON   *Dashiell Hammett*

1930   201 pages, Pan, £3.50 paperback

Not considered the best of Hammett's small output of novels, this nonetheless exemplifies many of the characteristics which illuminate his work. Sam Spade, disillusioned, isolated and tough, sets out to discover who killed the partner he did not even like very much, motivated by a sense of belief in the natural order of the universe and a determination to restore it as a small dam against encroaching chaos.

11. THE FRANCHISE AFFAIR   *Josephine Tey*

1948   254 pages, Penguin, £3.99 paperback

As a detective novel this perhaps does not rank among the best, but nonetheless it remains compelling because of its description of small-town life and its acutely-drawn characters. In the portrait of Betty, the young girl at the heart of the affair, Tey chillingly demonstrates the ease with which the devious can manipulate the innocent.

12. LAST SEEN WEARING . . .   *Hillary Waugh*

1952   Out of print

A classic of the police procedural genre, a straightforward investigation innocent of subplot or other fictional distractions. The mystery of a young girl's death in small-town America is meticulously analysed and its solution rigorously pursued; the suspense is beautifully sustained by a series of alternative explanations of what happened, each of which is in turn discarded until the truth is discovered.

13. THE NAME OF THE ROSE   *Umberto Eco*

1980   502 pages, Picador, £5.99 paperback

Take a Benedictine monastery in mediaeval Italy, add a handful of gruesome murders, a philosophical Franciscan sleuth, a detailed portrait of a closed society, some humour, some metaphysics, a lot of erudition and a thrilling climax and you have some of what the author has managed to enclose between the covers of this extraordinary and complex novel.

14. ROGUE MALE   *Geoffrey Household*

1939   192 pages, Penguin, £2.99 paperback

Hunter and hunted exchange roles as they stalk each other throughout this tense, relentless tale of a man who attempts to assassinate a European dictator (never mentioned, but strongly Hitlerian) and is eventually forced to go literally to earth before the final confrontation. The process of the hero's gradual reduction into an almost animal state as he lies holed up in his burrow is unforgettable.

15. THE LONG GOODBYE   *Raymond Chandler*

1953   320 pages, Penguin, £4.99 paperback

We read Chandler today as much for the evocation of the seedy side of California in the thirties and forties as for the plot. Philip Marlowe, the cynical fearless PI with a wisecrack and a butt perpetually dangling from his lip, became step-father to a multitude of similar tough-guy heroes who continue to investigate corruption – usually among the rich – armed with nothing but their slightly-dented ideals and a stern disregard for the trappings of wealth.

16. MALICE AFORETHOUGHT   *Francis Iles*

1931   236 pages, Dent, £3.95 paperback

As with *The Murder of Roger Ackroyd*, this novel appeals for its break-away from the detective story traditions of its time. From the opening sentence, both murderer and intended victim are known: the fascination lies in watching how it is dun, rather than who dun it. Thus character and psychology become as important a part of the plot as the crime itself.

The CWA's Favourite Male Writers:

1. Reginald Hill
2. Colin Dexter
3. Dick Francis
4. Raymond Chandler
5. Arthur Conan Doyle
6. Simon Brett
7. Georges Simenon
8. Eric Ambler
9. Elmore Leonard
10. John le Carré

Ed McBain
12. Julian Symons
Peter Dickinson
14. John Dickson Carr
15. Michael Innes
16. Edmund Crispin
17. Graham Greene
Peter Lovesey
19. Nicholas Freeling
Robert Barnard

---

17. THE DAY OF THE JACKAL   *Frederick Forsyth*

1971   412 pages, Corgi, £3.99 paperback

A man alienated from his own society decides to kill General de Gaulle. The reader follows along as he moves with ruthless professionalism from one stage to the next – the false passport, the evasion of pursuers, the construction of a rifle that will pass undetected through the security checks – in his attempt to commit the perfect assassination. So enthralling is this story that however many times one reads it, one still wonders with a frisson whether this time he'll make it.

18. THE NINE TAILORS *Dorothy L. Sayers*

1934   299 pages, Coronet, £2.99 paperback

It is always disapprovingly said of Dorothy Sayers that she was in love with her own creation. What's wrong with that? Despite his many absurdities, Lord Peter Wimsey remains one of the most endearing of amateur sleuths. One of Sayers' achievements in the corpus of her work is the protracted love affair between Harriet Vane and Lord Peter, as both characters develop over time.

The Nine Tailors owes much of its popularity to the author's specialised knowledge of campanology – how many of us owe all we shall ever know about bell-ringing to an early acquaintance with this book? A brutally beaten corpse is discovered in the churchyard of a small East Anglian village and Lord Peter Wimsey, using the intricacies of change-ringing, comes up with the culprit. The descriptions of the kind of lonely fenlands where Sayers grew up are particularly effective.

19. AND THEN THERE WERE NONE *Agatha Christie*

1939 (as TEN LITTLE NIGGERS)   281 pages, Fontana, £3.25 paperback

Ten guests who have no apparent connection with each other are invited to stay on an island by a host who fails to show up – or so it seems. When they start getting bumped off one by one, it becomes apparent that the host is one of them and, what's more, has a grudge against each one. For Christie fans, this is one of her most intriguing puzzles – and one of the few in which there is no Poirot or Marple on hand to solve the murders.

20. THE THIRTY-NINE STEPS *John Buchan*

1915   138 pages, Pan, £3.50 paperback

A very English gentleman pits his wits against the unspeakable Hun: no prizes for guessing who comes out on top. Despite anachronisms, this is still one of the finest chase stories around.

21. THE COLLECTED SHERLOCK HOLMES SHORT STORIES   *Arthur Conan Doyle*

1892–1927   285 pages, Penguin, £2.99 paperback

A collective CWA vote for the unsurpassed stories on which most crime writers were weaned. They're all here: *The Red-Headed League, The Sussex Vampire, His Last Bow, The Dancing Men, The Musgrave Ritual, The Five Orange Pips,* etc, etc. This volume never leaves my bedside, *The Lion's Mane* and *The Speckled Band* remaining constant favourites. Sherlock Holmes himself has featured so often on the screen that we all feel we know him intimately, yet Conan Doyle's achievement was to create a character at once familiar and yet always aloof, distanced from the reader not only by his mighty brain-power but also his dissolute, even warped personality.

22. MURDER MUST ADVERTISE   *Dorothy L. Sayers*

1933   288 pages, Coronet, £3.50 paperback

A man is killed falling down a steep flight of stairs in a seedy advertising agency; his replacement turns out to be none other than Peter Wimsey. Although the author draws extensively on her own experiences as a copywriter in just such a firm, it is hard to imagine her involved with the flighty, drug-taking crowd with which she peoples these pages.

The CWA's Favourite Female Writers:

1. Ruth Rendell
2. Dorothy L. Sayers
3. Agatha Christie
4. P.D. James
5. Josephine Tey
6. Margery Allingham
7. Patricia Highsmith
8. Emma Lathen
9. Sue Grafton
10. Sara Paretsky
11. June Thomson
12. Sarah Caudwell
    Barbara Vine
14. Ngaio Marsh
15. Margaret Millar
16. Paula Gosling
17. Susan Moody
18. Christianna Brand
19. Ellis Peters
20. Celia Fremlin

---

23. TALES OF MYSTERY AND IMAGINATION
Edgar Allan Poe

1852   592 pages, Dent, £4.50 paperback

The models for numerous subsequent detective stories, containing in particular the first 'Watson' and the first great serial sleuth. Like so many who followed, the Chevalier Auguste Dupin was fantastically intelligent, incredibly cultured, and unfailingly contemptuous of the police. *The Murders in the Rue Morgue* remains for many the classic short detective story; *The Purloined Letter* is equally popular.

23. THE MASK OF DIMITRIOS   *Eric Ambler*

1939   268 pages, Fontana, £2.95 paperback

A crime novelist turned detective follows the trail of a supposedly dead man back into a sordid chain of politics, assassination, drug-running, double-cross and white slavery. As with *The Day of the Jackal*, the remorseless build-up of convincing detail adds to the tension of this first-class thriller.

23. THE MOVING TOYSHOP   *Edmund Crispin*

1946   205 pages, Penguin, £3.99 paperback

Perhaps the best of Crispin's small but original *oeuvre* of humorous detective fiction. Gervase Fen, his irrepressible professor hero, remains one of the most charming of sleuths. Here, Fen investigates the mysterious mobility of an Oxford toyshop in his usual flippantly literate way.

26. THE TIGER IN THE SMOKE   *Margery Allingham*

1952   272 pages, Hogarth Press, £4.95 paperback

Suspenseful and sinister, this novel remains the best example of a perhaps somewhat underrated author's work. Yet another hunter and hunted tale, containing much murky atmosphere and some fine big-city observation. Containing, too, Albert Campion, her perennially popular detective, who began as a bit of a Wimsey clone, lightweight and two-dimensional, but who gradually evolved into something rather more shrewd and serious, eventually becoming a mouthpiece for Allingham herself.

27. THE FALSE INSPECTOR DEW *Peter Lovesey*

1982   251 pages, Arrow, £3.50 paperback

Gold Dagger–winning example of Lovesey's ability to recreate the past, the story is set in 1921 and has obvious parallels with the celebrated Crippen murder case, in which a mild-mannered little doctor killed his domineering wife and buried her remains in the cellar before fleeing for Canada with his mistress. Period London is wonderfully realised as is the elegance of life aboard a transatlantic liner. With murder and mystery thrown in for good measure, who could ask for more?

28. THE WOMAN IN WHITE *Wilkie Collins*

1860   648 pages, Penguin, £2.99 paperback

An ingeniously plotted tale of unlawful confinement in a lunatic asylum in order that an unscrupulous villain might falsely claim a large inheritance. More than that, however: in addition to the plot, the author produces some surprisingly memorable characters.

29. A DARK-ADAPTED EYE *Barbara Vine*

1986 300 pages, Penguin, £3.50 paperback

The first of the novels written by Ruth Rendell's alter ego, in which she brilliantly uses the don't-let's-talk-about-it hypocrisies of a more conventional era – the Fifties – to hide a dark family secret and create an atmosphere of almost unbearable tension.

30. THE POSTMAN ALWAYS RINGS TWICE
James M. Cain

1934 Included in The Five Great Novels of James M. Cain, *633 pages, Picador, £5.95 paperback*

Wife and lover plot to murder her husband: an old theme made memorable because handled with a taut economy of language and a sexual explicitness which caused offence at the time it appeared, though it seems fairly ordinary today. Remains a classic piece of hardboiled writing.

31. THE GLASS KEY *Dashiell Hammett*

1931 220 pages, Pan, £1.95 paperback

Generally considered Hammett's best, *The Glass Key* has been chosen by Julian Symons as the best crime novel ever written. An exploration of human relationships, an observation of the quirks of friendship, a study of the ambiguities of guilt and innocence. And also a cracking good tale of political corruption and gangsterism.

32. THE HOUND OF THE BASKERVILLES   *Arthur Conan Doyle*

1902   174 pages, Penguin, £2.99 paperback

The best of the full-length Holmes adventures, full of suspense, in which a gigantic dog terrorises the lonely Devon moors – or does it? Trust Holmes to sort things out.

33. TINKER, TAILOR, SOLDIER, SPY   *John le Carré*

1974   367 pages, Coronet, £4.50 paperback

Highly successful, complicatedly plotted, though containing too many *longeurs* for my taste, this novel shows a shift in perspective from the author's earlier work (*see No. 3 above*), with spying no longer simply a dirty business but also a game for patriots.

34. TRENT'S LAST CASE   *E. C. Bentley*

1913   Out of print

When it was published this book broke new ground by including not only a detective who gets things completely wrong but also a strong love interest. The murder of tycoon Sigsbee Manderson is lightheartedly investigated by journalist Philip Trent, a far cry from the infallible classic detective. This ironic look at the crime genre has remained a classic.

35. FROM RUSSIA WITH LOVE   *Ian Fleming*

1957   208 pages, Coronet, £2.50 paperback

James Bond at his smooth and unlikely best. Enormously popular at the time it came out, partly because the British public was at last able to draw a post-war breath and look around for some vicarious glamour and excitement. It was precisely this kind of pseudo-sophisticated spy story which prompted the gritty realism of le Carré and Deighton.

36.= COP HATER   *Ed McBain*

1956   171 pages, Penguin, £2.75 paperback

This book stands for all the 87th Precinct novels, which feature the team of cops led by Steve Carella. Apparently authentic police procedure, crackling dialogue and the careful individualisation of each of the men of the 87th have turned the series into a global success. In this one, someone is knocking off the cops themselves. *Sadie When She Died* (*see No. 96*) and *Hail, Hail, The Gang's All Here* also notched up a considerable number of votes from the CWA.

36.= THE DEAD OF JERICHO   *Colin Dexter*

1981   224 pages, Pan, £3.99 paperback

One of a series set in Oxford and featuring the morose yet likeable Inspector Morse. The plots are craftily ingenious, the characters convincing. It is perhaps a little difficult now for anyone possessing a TV set to visualise Morse separate from the character as played in the excellent television series.

38. STRANGERS ON A TRAIN *Patricia Highsmith*

1950   256 pages, Penguin, £3.50 paperback

Two young men meet on a train. One offers to murder someone the other wishes dead in return for the same favour. Since the connections between the two are entirely random, this ought to be the perfect crime. However . . . One of Highsmith's disturbing psychological explorations of the ordinary human psyche in the grip of obsession, this chilling story, turned by Alfred Hitchcock into one of the finest of suspense films, amply illustrates the author's stated belief that the writer of suspense 'should throw some light on his characters' minds.'

39. JUDGEMENT IN STONE *Ruth Rendell*

1977   191 pages, Arrow, £3.50 paperback

A family is gunned down by their illiterate housekeeper and her friend, the mentally unstable Joan Smith, who sees herself as the instrument of the Lord. Why did it happen? Beautifully interlocking plot, and the kind of build-up towards inescapable horror that is this writer's forte.

40. THE HOLLOW MAN (published in New York as THE THREE COFFINS) *John Dickson Carr*

1938   256 pages, Penguin, £3.99 paperback

The master of the 'impossible' crime here includes a learned dissertation by his serial sleuth, the imposing Dr. Gideon Fell, on the different ways a locked-room murder may be set up. One of the prime examples of the author's skill in presenting and then unravelling obfuscation for the marvelling reader.

John Dickson Carr wrote a great number of ingeniously plotted crime puzzles under this and other names, the most notable of which was Carter Dickson. His particular skill was sleight-of-pen and audience-deception, and his ability to point the reader in the wrong direction. *The Judas Window* (1938), which was another locked room mystery, also received a large number of votes.

41. THE POISONED CHOCOLATES CASE *Anthony Berkeley*

1929   Out of print

A murder is committed via a box of poisoned chocolates; a Chief Inspector describes the case to six connoisseurs of crime who then offer their own widely differing solutions. An innovation in the crime novel in that it not only poked fun at contemporary crime fiction, which was beginning to take itself a little too seriously, but also did not allow the author's protagonist, Roger Sheringham, to come up with the correct solution. Anthony Berkeley also wrote as Francis Iles (*see No. 16*).

42. = A MORBID TASTE FOR BONES

1977   192 pages, Futura, £2.99 paperback

42. = THE LEPER OF ST. GILES   *Ellis Peters*

1981   223 pages, Futura, £3.50 paperback

Ellis Peters' twelfth-century sleuthing monk, Brother Cadfael, is possibly the most popular detective currently being published in Britain. The attraction of the series derives both from the historical setting – mediaeval Shrewsbury, minutely if slightly romantically drawn – and from the worldly charm and character of Cadfael himself. In *A Morbid Taste for Bones*, Cadfael's first outing, he is called from the peace of his herbarium to solve the mystery surrounding a saint's bones; while in *The Leper of St. Giles*, one of Peters' very best, a young man accused of murder and seeking sanctuary from a mob asks for Cadfael's help to prove his innocence. (*Andrew Holgate*)

44. A KISS BEFORE DYING   *Ira Levin*

1953   223 pages, Pan, £3.99 paperback

An intricate novel of deception – the reader's – with an ingenious three-way look at murder. A girl is murdered by her boyfriend, but the murderer's identity is withheld until halfway through the book; the last third is a dramatic chase to the death of an arrogant killer. Levin cannot be described as a crime novelist (he later wrote *Rosemary's Baby* and *The Stepford Wives*) but with this book he gave the genre one of its most exciting examples.

45. THE TALENTED MR. RIPLEY   *Patricia Highsmith*

1955   249 pages, Penguin, £3.50 paperback

A study of a charming psychopath who murders a rich friend and adopts his identity. Remarkable because the author manages to make her conscienceless hero strangely fascinating, even attractive, perhaps because Tom Ripley manages to ignore the conventions which keep society functioning in a way that we all occasionally fantasise about doing but are mostly too afraid to do ourselves.

46. BRIGHTON ROCK   *Graham Greene*

1938   247 pages, Penguin, £3.50 paperback

Is this a crime novel? More a study in psychopathology, but none the less gripping for that. Pinkie, the young gangster protagonist, engages the sympathies of the reader despite his crimes, and the seedy world he inhabits rings with authenticity. In particular, this book illustrates one of Greene's recurring themes: that of the outcast pitted against the society he has rejected.

47. THE LADY IN THE LAKE   *Raymond Chandler*

1943   238 pages, Penguin, £4.99 paperback

World-weary PI Philip Marlowe is asked to track down a hard-drinking shoplifting wife who has gone missing, but instead finds someone else's wife dead in a lake. More dirt and darkness beneath the bright Californian sunshine, more mean streets for Philip Marlowe to go down, with his 'disgust for sham and a contempt for pettiness'.

48. PRESUMED INNOCENT   *Scott Turow*

1987   423 pages, Penguin, £4.99 paperback

Winner of the 1987 CWA Silver Dagger, this is an engrossing exposé of crime, politics and the US judicial system. A beautiful attorney is murdered in her own apartment: in the course of solving the crime the reader is treated to a highly unusual tale elegantly told, with a cast of compelling characters and some terrific twists and turns. His new novel – *Burden of Proof* – is plotted with equal complexity and places a minor character from the first book at the centre of a story of high finance and the law.

49. A DEMON IN MY VIEW   *Ruth Rendell*

1976   184 pages, Arrow, £3.50 paperback

Two men with very similar names are tenants in the same converted house; each struggles with a personal demon. One's affair with a married woman has reached the point of no return; the other's shop-window dummy has been removed from the cellar where he keeps it in order to strangle it when the urge takes him. The psychology of a murderer is studied in great detail and with the author's particular brand of compassion which makes it impossible for the reader to condemn the flawed human beings about whom she writes so compellingly.

50. = THE DEVIL IN VELVET *John Dickson Carr*

1951 Out of print

Mix together historical setting, a bargain with the Devil and a spot of time travelling and you have an unusual murder mystery which remains consistently popular.

50. = A FATAL INVERSION *Barbara Vine*

1987 317 pages, Penguin, £3.50 paperback

In 1986 the skeletons of a woman and a child are discovered in the grounds of a country mansion and the reader is transported back ten years to learn something of the events leading up to their deaths. Another superb Vine novel, distinguished both for the quality of the writing and the way the slow unravelling of the plot mirrors the long slow summer of 1976, which the author describes with a compulsive sense of place and time.

52. THE JOURNEYING BOY *Michael Innes*

1949 336 pages, Penguin, £3.99 paperback

The adolescent son (like our own Adrian Mole, a fancier of bad girls and worse poetry) of a world-famous scientist travels with his holiday tutor to Ireland and finds himself caught up in a tasty mishmash of spies, double identities, ocean caves and inept villains, all served up with dollops of wit and flair.

The CWA's Favourite Male Detectives

1. Inspector Morse — (Colin Dexter)
2. Sherlock Holmes — (Arthur Conan Doyle)
3. Lord Peter Wimsey — (Dorothy L. Sayers)
4. Philip Marlowe — (Raymond Chandler)
5. Albert Campion — (Margery Allingham)
6. Andrew Dalziel & Peter Pascoe — (Reginald Hill)
7. Hercule Poirot — (Agatha Christie)
8. Nero Wolfe — (Rex Stout)
9. Adam Dalgleish — (P.D. James)
10. Inspector Ganesh Ghote — (H.R.F. Keating)
11. Inspector Maigret — (Georges Simenon)
12. Charles Paris — (Simon Brett)
13. Father Brown — (G.K. Chesterton)
14. Gervase Fen — (Edmund Crispin)
15. Dr. Gideon Fell — (John Dickson Carr)

53. A TASTE FOR DEATH   *P.D. James*

1986   513 pages, Penguin, £4.99 paperback

Inspector Adam Dalgleish, poetry-writing protagonist of several of the author's highly regarded novels, here finds himself up to his neck in a convoluted mystery which begins with two blood-soaked bodies lying in the vestry of a London church. Far more than a finely worked-out mystery is offered: in the book's 513 pages the author ranges over a wide field and includes discussions of some of her own enthusiasms: church architecture, the meaning of faith, music, London itself.

54. THE EAGLE HAS LANDED   *Jack Higgins*

1975   383 pages, Pan, £3.99 paperback

An ill-assorted bunch of misfits, backed up by a team of German paratroopers, embark in 1943 on a mission to capture Churchill and hand him over to the Germans. In the traditional British manner, luck, pluck and inspiration win the day and thwart the Eagles at the last minute. Pacy writing and a fast moving plot, allied to some good characterisation and a believable love story, make this a winner.

55. MY BROTHER MICHAEL   *Mary Stewart*

1960   254 pages, Coronet, £2.99 paperback

As Paula Gosling has asked elsewhere in this volume, why are novels which fall into the 'romantic suspense' category so often ignored by the critics? They are no more or less formulaic than a police procedural or spy thriller, and often better written. Mary Stewart is one of the best in the genre, with a sense of place that lingers long after the book has been read. Her plots are always well-crafted and her characters intelligent. In *My Brother Michael* the heroine finds herself on Delphos, embroiled with a English schoolmaster anxious to discover the place where his brother died at the hands of Greek renegades – and something more. Stewart writes with passion about the landscapes of the country and interweaves her powerful story with references to the ancient gods whose presences still lie just below the surface of modern Greece.

56. = BERTIE AND THE TIN MAN *Peter Lovesey*

1987   230 pages, Arrow, £2.50 paperback

Subtitled *From the Detective Memoirs of King Edward VII*, this purports to be the story of how the then Prince of Wales turned amateur gumshoe in 1886 on hearing of the tragical suicide of Fred Archer, jockey. Highly diverting, the tale is told by the Prince himself, and shows him in wryly humorous vein, about himself, his Danish wife, his position as heir to the throne and above all, about his terrifying Mama, Queen Victoria.

56. = PENNY BLACK *Susan Moody*

1984   Out of print

A beautiful model is found murdered in the ladies washroom at Los Angeles airport. Penny Wanawake, six foot tall and sexy with it, sets out to discover who was responsible. The first in a series featuring the wisecracking black girl, this punchy novel received the kind of reviews authors would write for themselves if given the opportunity. (*Andrew Holgate*)

58. GAME, SET AND MATCH   *Len Deighton*

1984, 1985, 1986   Berlin Game *(1983), 325 pages, Grafton,*
£3.50 paperback; Mexico Set *(1984), 381 pages, Grafton, £3.50*
paperback; London Match *(1985), 405 pages, Grafton, £3.50*
paperback

Three books in one, this trilogy is set in Berlin, Mexico and
London, and stars Bernard Sampson, a former agent who
has spent the last five years behind a desk but is the only
man able to bring one defector over the Wall from East
Berlin, 'enrol' another seen in Mexico and, in the third
book, get him to talk when a KGB agent makes the kind
of confession which sets cats among pigeons. The usual
richly powerful mixture of action, authenticity and bleak
betrayal.

59. THE DANGER   *Dick Francis*

1983   286 pages, Pan, £3.99 paperback

I find this the best of the entire Dick Francis *oeuvre*; taut,
moving and crammed with excitement. Contains everything you could ever wish to know about the psychological
effects on those who find themselves caught up in what
must be one of the most cowardly of crimes. Horses are
more or less incidental in this entirely gripping tale.

60. DEVICES AND DESIRES   *P. D. James*

1989   408 pages, Faber & Faber, £6.99 paperback

Big enough to be a blockbuster rather than a crime novel, there is a bit of everything here: discos, drugs and terrorism, plus the author's usual penetrating and compassionate analysis of human frailties. A complex plot is enhanced by a perceptive and sensitive style.

61. UNDERWORLD   *Reginald Hill*

1988   351 pages, Grafton, £3.50 paperback

A missing girl, a fatal fall down a mineshaft, class antagonism and Dalziell and Pascoe; what more could any reader ask for? Hill's great strength lies in his ability to create a real and contemporary north-of-England background, far removed from the traditions of grey middleclassness which permeate so much crime fiction.

62. NINE COACHES WAITING   *Mary Stewart*

1958   317 pages, Coronet, £3.99 paperback

An updated version of the governess-in-distress story, with the heroine in love with a man she suspects may be trying to kill the child in her care. As usual with this author, the romantic interest is integral to the suspense and love always finds a way to unmask the true villain.

63. A RUNNING DUCK   *Paula Gosling*

1978   202 pages, Pan, £2.50 paperback

Winner of the John Creasey Memorial Prize for the best
first crime novel in 1978. A girl stops to help a man who
turns out to be a highly paid professional killer. Now that
she can identify him, he is bound to attempt to eliminate
her – which means the police can catch up with him at last.
The story contains elements of the disillusioned espionage
story (the 'goodies' are as ruthless as the 'baddies') and of
the classic chase, with the girl caught dangerously in the
middle. A very exciting debut.

64. SMALLBONE DECEASED   *Michael Gilbert*

1950   240 pages, Dent, £3.95 paperback

A corpse is found in a solicitor's office, stuffed into an air-
tight deedbox. Who, among the legal eccentrics attached to
the firm of Horniman, Birley & Crane, could have done it?
The professional background is impeccably observed, as
one would expect from a writer who was himself a prac-
tising solicitor.

65. THE ROSE OF TIBET   *Lionel Davidson*

1962   Out of print

An unashamed adventure story set against a background
which few know anything about and which is therefore
all the more mysterious. But Davidson is an accomplished
teller of other tales as well. Though far from prolific, he

has produced a consistently high standard of stylish work which, while predominantly suspenseful, falls into various categories. *The Night of Wenceslas* is a spy story of a kind; *Smith's Gazelle* is something quite different, a compelling story about the preservation of a herd of almost extinct deer. All his work is distinguished by an individual blend of warmth and sinewy strength.

66. INNOCENT BLOOD   *P. D. James*

1980   313 pages, Penguin, £3.99 paperback

An adopted child exercises her right to find out who her real parents are, and finds herself plunged into a nightmare of guilt and vengeance which leads inexorably to tragedy. One of the author's very best.

67. STRONG POISON   *Dorothy L. Sayers*

1930   224 pages, Coronet, £2.99 paperback

Up on a charge of murdering her lover, this is the first time Harriet Vane appears in Wimsey's (or our) life. Across a crowded courtroom their eyes meet and Wimsey falls in love – though it takes several more books before Harriet succumbs to his monocled blandishments – eventually getting her off through clever detection. Particularly interesting for the light it throws on the life of an unconventional bachelor girl in the Thirties.

68. HAMLET, REVENGE!   *Michael Innes*

1937   284 pages, Penguin, £3.99 paperback

Murder at a ducal seat during a staging of *Hamlet*,
providing plenty of opportunity for the urbanely donnish
Inspector Appleby to indulge in his penchant for literary
quotations while going about his lawful occasions and
bringing the culprit to book.

69. A THIEF OF TIME   *Tony Hillerman*

1989   209 pages, Sphere, £3.50 paperback

Since his first book appeared in 1970, Hillerman has
consistently received high praise for his series of novels set in Navajo Indian country and featuring Lt Joe
Leaphorn, of the Navajo Tribal Police, and Sergeant Jim
Chee. Despite the reviews, this is the first to hit the
really big time. As always, the ancient customs and
lore of a tribal reservation are shown in authentic and
moving detail and the relationship between the Navajo
and the harsh country they inhabit is beautifully realised.
Leaphorn and Chee have once again to juggle between the
differing demands of tribal and of federal law. Here, sacred
burial grounds are being violated, an anthropologist goes
missing and murder results from the attempt to cover up
the reasons. A compelling read.

70. A BULLET IN THE BALLET   *Caryl Brahms and S. J. Simon*

1937   159 pages, Hogarth Press, £4.95 paperback

Is this a detective novel? More of a pastiche for ballet-lovers, perhaps, as a series of Petroushkas are murdered and stolid Inspector Adam Quill is called in to clear the mystery up. The authors were good at conveying the behind-the-scenes frenzy of any theatrical performance.

71. DEAD HEADS   *Reginald Hill*

1983   320 pages, Grafton, £3.50 paperback

Most of Hill's crime novels feature the unlikely partnership of Superintendent Dalziel (crude and uncultured) and Sergeant Pascoe (sensitive and intellectual). Here, they are looking into the background of a rose-fancier who is 'a *real* gardener, rather than just a flash Harry wanting to put on a show' and who may also be a multiple murderer. As always, the novel contains some interesting characterisation, nice scene-setting and good writing, plus any number of horticultural tips.

72. THE THIRD MAN   *Graham Greene*

1950   157 pages, Penguin, £2.99 paperback

Greene called this 'an entertainment' and certainly it does not involve the classic elements of detective fiction; a crime, an investigation, a solution. Nor is it a novel of espionage, involving as it does not only the workings of intelligence operations in post-war Austria but also betrayal and disillusionment. The book is probably overshadowed by the famous film into which it was turned, in which the use of light and shadows evoked not only lost illusions but also the greater betrayals which Europe suffered in World War Two.

73. THE LABYRINTH MAKERS *Anthony Price*

1974   239 pages, Grafton, £2.95 paperback

It was a close thing between this book and the author's CWA Gold Dagger winner, *Other Paths to Glory*. This one was awarded the Silver Dagger, and finds bespectacled Dr. David Audley (the author's series hero) wondering why the Russians should be interested in the cargo of an RAF Dakota found lying in a Lincolnshire lake twenty-five years after the end of the Second World War. Wondering even more why he, an expert on the Middle East, should have been assigned to this particular case. As well as being an outstanding spy novelist, Price is particularly knowledgeable about both military history and archaeology, both of which interests he has drawn on to memorable effect in his work.

74. THE QUILLER MEMORANDUM *Adam Hall*

1965   Out of print

First of a series of books featuring Quiller, a trouble-shooting 'shadow-executive' working for a government agency so undercover that it does not officially exist, and possessed of specialised abilities which enable him to endure and survive against all odds – but only through intense observation at all times of what he calls 'the organism', i.e. his own body. High on suspense and action; at times the author's tongue appears to be firmly in his cheek.

75. BEAST IN VIEW   *Margaret Millar*

1955   160 pages, Penguin, £2.50 paperback

One of America's two leading ladies of crime, this is probably her best work. Contains a central plotting surprise that still continues to shock, although other authors have imitated it many times since. As always, the crime stretches back into the past; few writers convey the menace of inevitability as powerfully.

76. THE SHORTEST WAY TO HADES   *Sarah Caudwell*

1984   207 pages, Penguin, £2.99 paperback

The second in a series featuring a team of urbane young London barristers, lusty to a woman (let alone to a man), and their guru Professor Hilary Tamar. A large inheritance, a sailing accident in Greece and a considerable amount of classical mythology are stirred together and spiced with witty repartee and a delightfully mandarin style to form a delectable whole. The author produces at much too slow a pace for her many fans.

77. RUNNING BLIND   *Desmond Bagley*

1970   254 pages, Fontana, £2.99 paperback

A good example of Bagley's brand of fast-moving, non-stop action thrillers, which have made him probably the top British writer in the field. Set in Iceland, with plenty of weapon technology and background authenticity to make the reader feel Bagley knows exactly what he's writing about.

78. TWICE SHY   *Dick Francis*

1981   269 pages, Pan, £3.50 paperback

The mixture as always: horses, hero-with-handicap (child-lessness, in this case), technical knowhow on some esoteric subject (computer programming) and an interesting crime (a fraudulent betting system) plus fast-moving action and pacy writing. While this does not always match up to the best of Francis' own very high standard, it never fails to grip.

79. THE MANCHURIAN CANDIDATE
   Richard Condon

1959   285 pages, Arrow, £2.95 paperback

Must rank among the foremost of psychological thrillers. A GI captured by the Koreans is brainwashed and pro-grammed into becoming an assassin-in-waiting, a deadly weapon ready to kill on command. Things begin to go very wrong when the weapon's loved ones become involved. A first-rate story that is both action-packed and, at the same time, moving.

The CWA's Favourite Female Detectives:

1. Miss Jane Marple   (Agatha Christie)
2. Penelope Wanawake   (Susan Moody)
3. Cordelia Gray   (P.D. James)
4. Anna Lee   (Lisa Cody)
5. Kinsey Milhone   (Sue Grafton)
6. Jemima Shore   (Antonia Fraser)
7. V.I. Warshawski   (Sara Paretsky)
8. Dame Beatrice Bradley   (Gladys Mitchell)
9. Miss Silver   (Patricia Wentworth)
10. Harriet Vane   (Dorothy L. Sayers)
11. Mrs Pargeter   (Simon Brett)
12. Sarah Kelling   (Charlotte McLeod)
13. Inspector Charmian Daniels (Jenny Melville)
14. Professor Kate Fansler   (Amanda Cross)
15. Bertha Cool   (A.A. Fair)

---

80. THE KILLINGS AT BADGER'S DRIFT   *Caroline Graham*

1987   264 pages, Headline, £2.99 paperback

The first appearance of the appealing Detective Chief Inspector Barnaby won all kinds of praise from the reviewers and is a first-class example of the particularly English brand of whodunnit which the Americans call a 'cosy'. Elderly Miss Simpson is looking for a rare wild orchid when she sees something nasty in the wood. When she is later found dead in her sitting room, her bossy friend

Miss Bellringer refuses to believe that the causes were natural and Barnaby is reluctantly landed with the case. Witty writing and excellent characterisation enhance this close-up look at the dark side of village life; the second book in the series is even better.

81. THE BEAST MUST DIE   *Nicholas Blake*

1938   204 pages, Hogarth Press, £4.95 paperback

In amateur detective Nigel Strangeways, the author created a truly literary detective, rather than a mere spouter of apposite quotes like Appleby or Fen – as one might have expected, considering that a Poet Laureate lurks behind the pseudonym. As so many amateurs tend (need?) to be, Strangeways is on good terms with someone at the Yard, which is particularly helpful when he becomes involved with crime. This one is considered the best of a pretty good *oeuvre*.

81. GORKY PARK   *Martin Cruz Smith*

1981   335 pages, Fontana, £3.99 paperback

Somewhat densely written for this particular reader's taste and certainly far too long, this extraordinarily popular thriller nonetheless received all sorts of accolades from those who are supposed to know what they are talking about. It would be interesting to analyse the CWA's response and see what ratio of male to female votes were awarded to it. Three shot and mutilated bodies are found frozen beneath ice in Moscow's Gorky Park: why? Some nice East/West ideological confrontation and a reassurance that bureaucracy functions in the same inefficient manner whichever side of the Iron Curtain it exists.

83. DEATH COMES AS THE END   *Agatha Christie*

1945   219 pages, Fontana, £3.25 paperback

A Christie curio in more ways than one: not only is the book set in Egypt 4000 years ago – the family at the centre of the book nevertheless bearing a reassuring resemblance to many an English middleclass rural household – but it boasts the highest number of murders (8) of any Christie domestic crime novel. Despite the exotic location and the rapid rate of death, the book is not considered one of Christie's strongest. (*Andrew Holgate*)

84. GREEN FOR DANGER   *Christianna Brand*

1945   188 pages, Pandora, £3.95 paperback

Considered by many to be the author's best book, this ingenious plot concerns a murder which takes place on the operating table of a military hospital during World War Two in front of seven witnesses. Humorously, even facetiously written.

85. TRAGEDY AT LAW   *Cyril Hare*

1942   290 pages, Faber & Faber, £2.95 paperback

A circuit judge who has gazed upon the wine when it was red, and gone on gazing much longer than is wise, hits a

pedestrian. This is a fine legal detective story, acknowledged by the pundits to be a masterpiece of its kind. One
of a distinguished body of lawyer-authors, Hare wrote out
of first-hand experience, having been called to the Bar and
himself toured the circuit as a county court judge.

86. THE COLLECTOR   *John Fowles*

1963   277 pages, Pan, £3.99 paperback

Though the author does not count as a crime writer, this is
nonetheless a chilling story of kidnap and death. A speci-
men is observed in her local habitat and finally netted, to
be whisked away to a terrifying underground version of
a killing-bottle. As with most collectors, there is no intention of unkindness, which makes the tale all the more
frightening. No happy endings here, unfortunately.

87. GIDEON'S DAY   *J. J. Marric*

1955   Out of print

This stands for any one of a number of top-quality police
procedurals featuring Commander George Gideon of Scotland Yard, produced by the phenomenal John Creasey. The
series stands out from the rest of the author's vast output
for its air of authenticity and the ability to disguise the
fact, without hiding it, that for the most part police routine
is pretty dull stuff. The series was innovative at the time
in cutting from one case to another as each progressed:
this particular day of Gideon's involved drugs, theft, gang
warfare and murder.

88. THE SUN CHEMIST   *Lionel Davidson*

1976   Out of print

Among the papers of a noted scientist is a formula which could provide an alternative fuel source and so release its possessors from the need to buy oil from not always friendly neighbours. Quite apart from the plot, Davidson is always a splendid read, both for the jokes and for the rich world he is so good at creating.

89. THE GUNS OF NAVARONE   *Alistair Maclean*

1957   255 pages, Fontana, £2.50 paperback

Five men set out on a dangerous assignment: to silence the guns of Navarone, manned by the Germans and commanding the escape route of twelve hundred British troops. Tough, exciting adventure by a master of the genre.

90. THE COLOUR OF MURDER   *Julian Symons*

1957   192 pages, Papermac, £3.95 paperback

The CWA awarded its Gold Dagger to this novel about an ordinary man living in a dull suburb with an unsympathetic wife. Frustration leads him to fantasise about the local librarian: inevitably murder ensues. Symons is a master at investing the ordinary with menace and turning suburban landscapes into outposts of hell.

91. GREENMANTLE *John Buchan*

1916 Out of print

Another adventure for Richard Hannay, in which his brief is to prevent the Germans from resurrecting a prophet of Islam for their own dastardly ends. As Buchan himself wrote: 'Let no man or woman call its events improbable.'

Favourite Androgynous Detective

1. Professor Hilary Tamar (Sarah Caudwell)

---

92. THE RIDDLE OF THE SANDS *Erskine Childers*

1903 268 pages, Dent, £3.50 paperback

Two young men on a sailing holiday among the Friesian islands discover German plans to assemble a fleet with which to launch an invasion of England. Plenty of detail drawn from the author's own yachting experience, and some good evocative atmosphere. The remorseless build-up of suspicion and detail make this a classic in the action/adventure genre.

93. WOBBLE TO DEATH *Peter Lovesey*

1970 Out of print

The first of this popular author's recreations of a past age, this novel introduces the Victorian partnership of

Sergeant Cribb and Constable Thackeray, who find themselves involved in a phenomenon of the age – the marathon walk, or 'wobble' – in which one of the participants is murdered. The author says of his own work that he thinks of them as Victorian police-procedural novels and, as such, they provide a very satisfying read, full of historical detail yet maintaining a contemporary lightness of touch.

94. RED HARVEST   *Dashiell Hammett*

1929   Included in The Four Great Novels, *784 pages, Picador, £7.99 paperback.*

The first of Hammett's hardbitten novels with the Continental Op as protagonist. Here, the Op is assigned to clean up Personville, a town beset by feuding gangsters, and discovers that where violence and corruption are concerned, the only difference between cops and crooks is the cut of their suits. Riding out of town with the gangs temporarily out of business, he knows, in his world-weary way, that give the place a year or two and it will again be as bad as he found it.

95. THE KEY TO REBECCA   *Ken Follett*

1980   341 pages, Corgi, £2.99 paperback

Someone is secretly broadcasting British troop movements to the Germans and the whole British campaign in North Africa is at stake. Major Vandam, of Army Intelligence, and a beautiful local girl called Elene are the only ones who can stop the dangerous leaks. *Rebecca*, the novel by Daphne du Maurier (*see No. 6 above*) is the key to the whole affair. A thrilling book, packed with increasing tension as spy and spy-catcher come ever closer to a final denouement.

96. SADIE WHEN SHE DIED   *Ed McBain*

1972   Out of print

Further tales from the 87th Precinct (*see No. 36 above*), where detectives Kling and Carella, investigating the gruesome murder of a woman, find themselves making Suspect Number One a husband who finds it impossible to conceal his pleasure at her death. The fact that two McBain novels are represented in the Police Procedural Top Ten (*see page 69*) is ample testimony to his power and skill as a writer and to the enduring appeal of his 87th Precinct novels. (*Andrew Holgate*)

97. THE MURDER OF THE MAHARAJAH
  H.R.F. Keating

1980   223 pages, Arrow, £2.95 paperback

This non-Ghote book was awarded the Gold Dagger by the CWA, as much for its portrait of India in the Thirties as for its clever puzzle element. The Maharajah – a roguish fellow not above a little sly cheating at chess and the odd practical joke – is murdered; the crime must have been committed by one of a group of visitors to his palace. Full of good things.

98. WHAT BLOODY MAN IS THAT? *Simon Brett*

1987   184 pages, Futura, £2.95 paperback

Charles Paris, a slightly seedy actor always teetering on
the verge of 'resting', finds himself back in provincial
rep, playing most of the minor roles in 'the Scottish
play', from the Bleeding Sergeant to the Third Murderer.
In addition, he's trying to stay on the wagon – again.
When the fruity old ham playing Duncan is found dead
clutching an empty bottle of Courvoisier, Charles takes
on the additional part of amateur detective. Brett's inti-
mate knowledge of what goes on behind theatrical scenes,
the charm of his protagonist's character and the wit and
panache with which he writes make the Charles Paris
series unmissable.

98. SHOOTING SCRIPT *Gavin Lyall*

1966   234 pages, Coronet, £2.99 paperback

As a former Air Correspondent for *The Sunday Times*, Lyall
certainly knows about flying. Combining his expertise
with fast-paced, well-written plots has made him one of
the most popular writers of action thrillers. In this one,
Keith Carr, piloting cargo round the Carribean, finds himself mixed up with potentially lethal local politics.

100. THE FOUR JUST MEN *Edgar Wallace*

1906 Out of print

At one time, Wallace was producing one in every four books sold in England – and it shows. He did not have time to be a painstaking or meticulous writer, carrying his readers along with the sheer speed of action, his inventive imagination and the verve of his plotting. Here, four good men decide to take matters into their own hands when obviously guilty parties are able to escape the penalties of the law. But how did they manage to bump off the Foreign Secretary when he was in a locked room guarded by large numbers of Metropolitan policemen? You have to read to the end to find out – though readers who did that in 1906 in fact were thwarted by any lack of written solution, Wallace offering instead a prize of £500 to those who came up with the correct solution. It was not a publicity gimmick he repeated, since it nearly ruined him.

THE WORK OF THE FOLLOWING
RECEIVED LOTS OF VOTES
but no one book preponderated

Catherine Aird
Robert Barnard
Peter Dickinson
Nicholas Freeling
James McClure
Georges Simenon
June Thomson
John Wainwright
Joseph Wambaugh
Margaret Yorke

From the Rue Morgue to the Mean Streets. . . .

A guide to the different categories, discussed and assessed by ten current practitioners.

The section also includes the top ten books chosen within each category. Some books received votes across a number of different sections: the order of books listed in the ten categories may not therefore match the order within the 100 list. For an explanation of the selection process for the final listing, see the Introduction (page xii).

THE FOUNDING FATHERS

H.R.F. KEATING

THE TOP TEN:

1. THE MOONSTONE
Wilkie Collins (1868, 528 pages,
  Penguin, £2.99 paperback)

2. THE THIRTY-NINE STEPS
John Buchan (1915, 138 pages,
  Pan, £3.50 paperback)

3. THE COLLECTED SHERLOCK
HOLMES SHORT STORIES
Arthur Conan Doyle (1892–1927,
  285 pages, Penguin,
  £2.99 paperback)

4. TALES OF MYSTERY AND
IMAGINATION
Edgar Alan Poe (1852, 592 pages,
  Dent, £4.50 paperback)

5. THE WOMAN IN WHITE
Wilkie Collins (1860, 648 pages,
  Penguin, £2.99 paperback)

6. THE HOUND OF THE
BASKERVILLES
Arthur Conan Doyle (1902,
  174 pages, Penguin, £2.99
  paperback)

7. A STUDY IN SCARLET
Arthur Conan Doyle (1887, 135
  pages, Penguin, £2.50
  paperback)

8. TRENT'S LAST CASE
E.C. Bentley (1913,
  out of print)

9. BLEAK HOUSE
Charles Dickens (1853, 935
  pages, Penguin, £4.99
  paperback)

10. FATHER BROWN STORIES
(1929, 718 pages, Penguin,
  £6.99 paperback)

Wilkie Collins, sitting up there on his comfortably puffy cloud, his two simultaneous mistresses and their families happily grouped on clouds to either side, tortured no longer by the rheumatic gout that made him shriek as he dictated away (but, one hopes, as airily happy as he occasionally was from the opium he took for those fearful pains), will surely be delighted to hear that *The Moonstone* is, far and away, the top choice among the Founding Fathers of his followers in the art of crime writing. He always believed, as we do, that one should write for readers. 'Make 'em laugh, make 'em weep, make 'em wait.' That was his creed. And how it paid off in this most splendid book.

And, be it noted, Wilkie Collins does not appeal only to those readers of lower standards whom literary editors, sternly depressing crime reviews to the bottom of the page, and publishers, sloshing down a gun and a blonde on as many crime covers as they dare, believe to be the only people who buy our books. No, the great and formidable poet-guru T.S. Eliot has said of *The Moonstone*, not entirely accurately, that it is 'the first, the longest and the best of modern English detective stories' and dozens of the intelligentsia have echoed that praise.

But almost any praise you care to heap on *The Moonstone* – and, after reading it or re-reading, praise you will want to heap – will not be too fulsome. Collins, the pioneer, put into this book a great deal that we, creeping along behind him, have found reader-grabbing ever since. The story is a classic example of the innocent person who, against all odds, must be proved guiltless. Collins, too, actually made his detective, Sergeant Cuff, pronounce the words 'the pieces of the puzzle are not all put together.' And how many times we following writers have echoed them. And Cuff it was who said 'I have never met with such a thing as a trifle yet', while Sherlock Holmes himself could only parrot out: 'you know my method. It is founded upon the observance of –' Guess what. Cuff, with his talk of 'the dirtiest ways of this dirty little world', also even pre-figures Sam Spade and Marlowe. And with 'nobody has stolen the diamond' he marvellously antedates the mysterioso pronouncements of Hercule Poirot.

I go further even in my claims for *The Moonstone*. Surely Collins not only fathered the detective novel with this potent seed but he also produced the kind of book that we later writers in the field prided ourselves on having arrived at only in the latter half of the twentieth century, the crime novel. Because in its pages *The Moonstone* does everything that the novel pure does. It is full of fine, and deep, character studies and, more, it has a theme underlying it of everlasting significance. Collins in a hundred touches evokes for us the fearful irrational that lies, like the secret hidden under the quagmire of the Shivering Sands, beneath the rational surface we like to think that life consists of. So we read, we are gripped and entertained, and underneath we are made to learn about the terrible verities.

But, if *The Moonstone* leads the field as far ahead as was Dick Francis in the Grand National before his mount mysteriously collapsed, there are nine strong runners behind, including, coming in at a hard-galloping fourth, Collins' other masterwork, *The Woman in White*, with its unforgettable villain Count Fosco, he of the mouse-disporting waistcoat, and its less flamboyant but equally memorable portrait of Marian Halcombe, surely a predecessor of the indomitable female private eyes who are now popping up all over crime fiction.

But first of the pursuing thoroughbreds (in date well preceding *The Moonstone*) comes Edgar Allan Poe's *Tales of Mystery and Imagination*, though the bulk of those are not really our concern here. But three of them mightily are,

59

and perhaps two more. In *The Murders in the Rue Morgue*, *The Mystery of Marie Roget* and *The Purloined Letter* that extraordinary semi-genius Poe laid down for ever the parameters of the art of detection writing. He gave us, in Le Chevalier C. Auguste Dupin, the Great Detective, that figure combining in himself the two apparently opposed sides of our human nature, the poet and the mathematician, the intuiter and the rationalist. He created in him a grand hero of the Romantic Revolution. He aimed in giving Dupin to us to free us from the locked rooms of our preconceived ideas, the laid-down laws of the ancients (or the regulated activities of police detectives). Though we swallow his draught well mixed with strawberry flavouring, from what he struck out in thought we all benefit.

Yet perhaps we would not have done so were it not for the quietly decent G.P. who took the figure Poe had fashioned and fleshed it out as one Sherrinford Holmes, later Sherlock. Conan Doyle, supremely in *The Adventures of Sherlock Holmes*, gave us the Great Detective as memorable human being, if human being so far above most of us that we need a Dr Watson as a sort of step-ladder up to him. Sherlock had first seen the light in number seven in our Founding Fathers list, wherin we heard those magical words addressed to Dr Watson, 'you have been in Afghanistan, I perceive', prototypal demonstration of the ever-intriguing, ever-imitated method of the scientific consulting detective. But it is in this collection of twelve stories that Holmes properly established himself and won for detective writing, and for all of us who have produced sub-Sherlocks, anti-Sherlocks and sub-sub Sherlocks, our publics.

Conan Doyle, that simple G.P., also, deservedly, has a third runner in the Founding Fathers Stakes, the haunting *The Hound of the Baskervilles*. This triple Conan Doyle achieves, I surmise, from a quality about him that is not as much recognised as perhaps it might be. Seduced by the Holmesean method, we are apt to think his appearances in print achieve their success because of that, because of his brilliance in seeing the significance of the fact that the dog did not bark in the night-time.

But I believe that it is the sheer, quiet excellence of Doyle's writing that has preserved the tales of the great Sherlock in everlasting salt. You get it in those instant and memory-stamped characterisations (Dr Grimesby Roylott – what a splendid name – suddenly appearing in Holmes' rooms, 'his deep-set, bile-shot eyes, and his high thin fleshless nose, [giving] him somewhat the resemblance to a fierce old bird of prey') and you get it, less obviously, in the occasional marvellously telling phrase, such as the closing words of Chapter Six of *The Hound*: 'There came no other sound save the chiming clock and the rustle of the ivy on the wall.'

Four more horses for this course still running well, two of them perhaps that might have been entered for the Golden Age Challenge Cup, E.C. Bentley's *Trent's Last Case* and Buchan's *The Thirty-Nine Steps*, this latter indeed perhaps a runner in the Thriller Handicap.

Trent's Last Case is something of a comicality. It was written as a send-up of the already highly popular detective story. But, like a chap who visits a prostitute and finds he has fallen in love, Bentley proved to have written a book that has been hailed many times since as a classic of the genre, and with its introduction of the detective as Laughing Sleuth, and a fallible one, it certainly gave our art a new direction and one which many of us have happily gone along with since. While *The Thirty-Nine Steps*, though by no means the first adventure yarn (or 'shocker', as Buchan called it) to delight the public, is perhaps the best example we have of this sort of book, every subsequent attempt notwithstanding. Why otherwise does there exist that critic's staple adjective, buchanesque?

Which leaves me with two other runners to look over in the Ring, two very different quadrupeds but each a model of its kind. There is *Bleak House* (Charles Dickens up), more novel than crime story but with what the American short-story maestro Stanley Ellin called 'that streak of wickedness in human nature' permeating all, and giving us – ever to be grateful for – Inspector Bucket of the Detective, he of the powerfully wagging forefinger, prime contender as the first transfer of an investigator from real life into fiction.

And there is the *Father Brown Stories* (I was going to say, G.K. Chesterton up, but the thought of that massive bulk upon any beast beyond the ponderous pachyderm is altogether too much). Father Brown, first perhaps of the anti-detectives, what a delight he is with his round dumpling face in utter contrast to the hawk-like Holmesean features, with his religion – and real religion it always is – in blank opposition to the Holmesean science. And then there are the Chestertonian paradoxes, spitting and sparkling like a whole children's party of fireworks. What a gift to posterity. One to add to the nine that have gone before, a diadem of delights.

H.R.F Keating is a former chairman of the CWA and currently President of the Detection Club. His latest novel, The Iciest Sin *– once again featuring the redoutable Inspector Ghote – is published this autumn.*

THE GOLDEN AGE (1914–1939)

ROBERT BARNARD

THE TOP TEN:

1. THE MURDER OF ROGER ACKROYD
Agatha Christie (1926, 235 pages, Fontana, £3.25 paperback)

2. GAUDY NIGHT
Dorothy L. Sayers (1935, 446 pages, Coronet, £3.99 paperback)

3. THE NINE TAYLORS
Dorothy L. Sayers (1934, 299 pages, Coronet, £2.99 paperback)

4. AND THEN THERE WERE NONE
Agatha Christie (1939, 281 pages, Fontana, £3.25 paperback)

5. THE TIGER IN THE SMOKE
Margery Allingham (1952, 272 pages, Hogarth Press, £4.95 paperback)

6. THE HOLLOW MAN
John Dickson Carr (1938, 256 pages, Penguin, £3.99 paperback)

7. THE POISONED CHOCOLATES CASE
Anthony Berkeley (1929, out of print)

8. A BULLET IN THE BALLET
Caryl Brahms and S.J. Simon (1937, 159 pages, Hogarth Press, £4.95 paperback)

9. THE BEAST MUST DIE
Nicholas Blake (1938, 205 pages, Hogarth Press, £4.95 paperback)

10. THE JUDAS WINDOW
Carter Dickson (out of print)

The Golden Age of the detective story was inaugurated in 1920 with *The Mysterious Affair at Styles*. There had been precursors (of which E.C. Bentley's *Trent's Last Case* is perhaps the closest in form, style and feel), but it is appropriate to date the age from Agatha Christie's first book because she was the finest, the cunningest and the most fecund of all its practitioners.

It was from the first a fun genre – a form of escapism for a generation that had a great deal, both in the present and the immediate past, that it wanted to escape from. The form soon built up a series of rules and conventions – a framework for the puzzle which it was both fun to play within and fun, now and then, to break out of. The artificial, non-realistic nature of the stories, the sense of a form which is both braced and restricted by rules, makes the most obvious literary comparison that with Restoration comedy – another product of a war-weary generation. The Restoration writers played games of love, the post-war detective writers played games of death.

By the mid-1920s the detective story was one of the most popular forms of fiction, and it had a kind of respectability that the romance, say, or the thriller definitely lacked. It was generally assumed – with what truth it is impossible to say – that it was the relaxation of good minds. This was an idea that Edmund Wilson tried to demolish in 1944 with his essay 'Who Cares Who Killed Roger Ackroyd?', but his rabbit punch went wild. His question, in any case, was answered by the sales figures. It is answered once again by the book's position in this poll.

The success of Christie and Sayers in the early twenties spawned a host of followers and imitators. It is not to be wondered at that many of the books read pretty thinly today. What is surprising is that *all* of the crime novels of Christie and Sayers, Allingham and Marsh, are to this day more or less perpetually in print. There is no other popular writer of whom this could be said. The escapist urge that led readers to seek refuge from memories of trench warfare and the miseries of mass unemployment in the inter-war years in literature that resembles a stately, formalised dance around a mysteriously murdered corpse is still operative today. We still want to know whodunnit, and the masochistic side to our natures still wants the author to pull some outrageous trick that will show us that we have got all our presuppositions wrong.

Because if the conventions and restrictions of the genre are one part of its appeal – we feel *safe* with murder, a pleasurable paradox – the other part is the element of challenge. The writers put before us the elements of the puzzle and challenge us to reassemble them in a way that will give us the whole picture of the crime, and hence its solution. It is no accident that this was also the great age of the jigsaw puzzle and the crossword. Christie went further: her great productiveness, and a series of outrageous surprises that started with *Roger Ackroyd*, enabled her to build up a particular sort of relationship with her readers which was quite independent of media hype or signing sessions or any of the other trappings of modern literary success. 'Fool me!' pleaded her readers, rather like puppies rolling over on their backs to be tickled. And again and again Christie obliged.

It is notable that Christie's main detectives are both outsiders – in Poirot's case by virtue of his nationality, in both cases by virtue of their marital status. The unmarried person does not have the same stake in the community and its continued stability as the married one does – he is a spectator rather than a player. The other three star Golden Age writers chose detectives who are part of the community, indeed part of the Establishment. They are rebel members (Lord Peter by virtue of his levity and his learning, Alleyn by his profession, Campion by his somewhat informally-assumed role of private detective), but their attitudes are not significantly different from others in their social group, and they all end up married and the fathers of sons. If it was true, as Margery Allingham asserted with her tongue not too far from her cheek, that Campion's destiny was to inherit the throne of England, there is something slightly royal about all three, though they are perhaps closer to the House of Stuart than the House of Windsor.

Christie was a very well-read woman who did not let her learning seep into her books. Sayers consciously appealed to a better-read, more 'literary' audience, with a battery of cultural references and a more complex (some would say heavier) prose style. Her books are more varied, in that they rarely base their appeal solely on the question of who did it. Why, and in particular how, often interests Sayers more. The early Lord Peter has his irritating moments, even half-hours, but many find the early, more light-hearted books from the twenties more to their taste than the more complex, many-layered books from the thirties. Margery Allingham is also immensely various, ranging from the simple – though always lively and original – whodunnits such as *Police at the Funeral* to the eerie and complex chase story which is *Tiger in the Smoke*, with its demonically attractive hero-villain, a type she was particularly good at. What she excelled in (as Agatha Christie recognised in a generous tribute she paid her younger contemporary) was atmosphere: all the books have a different feel to them – they are unease-inducing, all of them, but in very different ways.

No Ngaio Marsh book gets on to the list of ten. I wonder why? She was prolific, beguiling, with consistently high standards, yet there is about the actual detection in her books an element of the plodding. Perhaps this has put off her fellow professionals of today. On the other hand, there is in the list ample acknowledgement of the fun element in crime fiction – an element which too many po-faced chroniclers have regretted or ignored. There is a fun element in almost all Golden Age novels, a dancing, laughing undercurrent, but in *The Poisoned Chocolates Case* and *Bullet in the Ballet* the fun element takes over almost entirely, and produces brilliantly elegant and very funny entertainments.

The top book in this category, *The Murder of Roger Ackroyd*, not only received most votes; it received twice as many as the next book on the list. The reader coming to the book for the first time (and the delightful thing about Golden Age books is how they can still entrance the young, and how new foreign markets are opening up to them all the time) might for much of its length feel some surprise at its status on the list. It seems like a very straightforward detective novel – country village, manor house, 'county' people, shifty butler, inarticulate military man, and so on. There's a new side-kick for Poirot, and a more agreeable, better-drawn one than Hastings, whose thickness was becoming counter-productive. So it is the ingredients as before – gossip, hints of love affairs, greed for money – and it is only as we approach the end that we begin to get inklings of what it is that is to give this particular novel its distinction in the Golden Age canon. It is not just that it has a wonderful surprise ending: so does *Crooked House, And Then There Were None, Hercule Poirot's Christmas*. This one has a surprise ending that changes our whole reading of the book. It is as if a sudden change of lighting makes everything on stage look different. It is a book which it is a particular pleasure to read for the second time, to appreciate the stylistic skill by which the sleight-of-hand is concealed.

Ten stylised, stylish masterpieces of crime and detection, by eight notable practitioners of the genre. We have superb crime writers today, yet one is bound to look at these figures, wonder at the sheer *amount* of wonderful entertainment they provided for readers, and muse: 'Here be giants'.

As well as his study of Agatha Christie, entitled A Talent to Deceive, *and a history of English literature, Robert Barnard has written twenty-four crime novels. He is currently on the committee of the CWA.*

POLICE PROCEDURAL

JOHN WAINWRIGHT

THE TOP TEN

1. LAST SEEN WEARING. . .
Hillary Waugh (1952, out of
    print)

2. COP HATER
Ed McBain (1956, 171 pages,
    Penguin, £2.75 paperback)

3. THE DEAD OF JERICHO
Colin Dexter (1981, 224
    pages, Pan, £3.99 paperback)

4. UNDERWORLD
Reginald Hill (1988, 351
    pages, Grafton, £3.50
    paperback)

5. DEAD HEADS
Reginald Hill (1983, 320
    pages, Grafton, £3.50
    paperback)

6. GORKY PARK
Martin Cruz Smith (1981, 335
    pages, Fontana, £3.99
    paperback)

7. GIDEON'S WAY
J.J. Marric (1955, out of print)

8. SADIE WHEN SHE DIED
Ed McBain (1972, out of print)

9. THE MURDER OF THE
    MAHARAJAH
H.R.F. Keating (1980, 223
    pages, Arrow, £2.95
    paperback)

10. THE ONION FIELD
Joseph Wambaugh (1975, 432
    pages, Futura, £2.50
    paperback)

THE ART IS NOT SO SIMPLE ANY MORE

If you seek the complete answer to Chandler's 'Man-With-A-Gun-In His-Hand' dictum, read Hillary Waugh's *Last Seen Wearing*.

H.R.F. Keating (who knows a good thing when he reads it) describes it as a classic. I agree. The story of a small-town, New England murder is as fastidiously detailed as a Fabergé miniature, yet it still has that 'smell of life' which is unique to the novel and which no stage-craft, no TV drama and no film script can equal.

It tops the heap in a bunch which includes McBain, Hill, Rendell and Wambaugh. No more need be said. It is a Police Procedural, and that might be a clue to the monumental gaff made by that Raymond of great and respected memory.

Raymond Chandler was top cat in the private eye industry of the 30s and 40s. His vehicle to the top was pulps – *Black Mask* and *Dime Detective* – and his attitude to writing was hooked onto the contemptuous, pulp-tough-guy attitude. His opinions were crisp, lucid and entertaining, but they were not always the opinions of Chandler the author. Very often they were the opinions of Philip Marlowe, the dry-witted, cynical and non-existent character who brought Chandler fame.

(This happens. The last time I saw Charteris, he still had a distinctly 'saintly' air. Long before Sean Connery moved onto the big screen, Fleming was an obvious double-zero candidate.)

Marlowe did not like cops. His Mean Street was peopled by crooked cops and minor corruption. The Bad Guys Mk.I were revealed at the denouement, but the Bad Guys Mk.II were around from page one and the Bad Guys Mk.II were in the force.

Having built a cloud-high reputation upon this bedrock

of belief, and despite having a warm spot for the men in blue at La Jolla, Chandler was barred from approving, or even officially acknowledging, the Police Procedural school of yarn telling.

Not that it mattered. At that time the sub-genre of Police Procedural was such a *rara avis* as to be almost invisible to the naked eye.

In this country, the 30s and 40s crimesters did the cops what they took to be a big favour. They acknowledged their existence. The Golden Age saw much mention of policemen. From Poirot (late of the Belgian Sureté) to the plodding and painfully correct Inspector French. Coppers and ex-coppers. They dug them up from all points of the compass. From Honolulu, Charlie Chan. From Kent, Inspector Cockrill. From Yorkshire, Sergeant Cluff. From New York, Inspector Queen. They came by the dozen. Many left, but more than a handful stayed, and some are still with us.

The trigger-action of the book was crime, and justice must prevail. Undiluted hooey was often fed to the readers, but the fuzz were around to give it pseudo-authenticity. And (sad, but true) too often the cop's other job was to amuse. A world was invented; a world of impossible policemen whose antics were directed at making the observer chuckle.

Murder had to be out, of course . . . but only eventually.

First came the regulation number of pages. Therein, the police hero ran grave risk of being certified because of personal foibles. He talked to himself too much. He was unnecessarily secretive. He was outrageously devious.

And, why?

To catch a 'master criminal' who, in the final analysis, had a permanent I.Q. of a blind drunk moron.

The wonder was that, despite such obstacles, the crime-reading public could justify its choice of literature to those who scorned.

Things were much simpler in those days. The average circulating library had but three classifications. 'Romance', 'Western' and 'Crime'. Everything fitted within those three sections. From P.G. Wodehouse to Edgar Wallace – from Defoe to Dickens – however much imagination was called for, it fitted in there, somewhere.

But still no readily recognisable Police Procedural.

Meanwhile, in Yorkshire – in Halifax Borough Police – a copper was feeling hard done by. The gentle nawpings of a provincial force upset Constable Procter and he voiced his objections. It had no real effect, other than to earn him a posting to a secluded beat, on the very fringe of Halifax, where he could do no harm and sit what remained of his service out without making a nuisance of himself.

Procter retaliated by writing two books, in quick succession. *No Proud Chivalry* and *Each Man's Destiny*. They had very heavy titles, but very light story lines, and they were not about crime. They were about a provincial police force and its various, minor corruptions. In effect, they were novelties, in that they were really about Halifax Borough and what was going on under the surface.

A little local hell popped, questions were asked in Parliament and Constable Procter was wise enough to tender his resignation while the spotlight kept him from any real harm.

He'd proved he could write, so he wrote. First, detective stories – the then normal and popular 'puzzle' yarns with a twist ending – then the penny dropped. Why not make the detective a *real* detective; the ranks, the authorities, the police back-up and the limited area in which various officers could claim power.

And that was it. The Police Procedural; born of fiddles, suckled on bitterness and arriving almost by mistake.

Maurice Procter wrote some good books – some very

readable Police Procedurals – before he died in 1973. The strange thing is the lack of credit pushed his way for introducing a new way of telling a crime yarn.

Nor was it an easy way of telling.

The top drawer of the old school had tried, for years, to show the workings of a criminal mind. The new school had the police mind to handle, too. Just as devious. Just as fascinating. And, if you doubt that, try Wambaugh's *The Onion Field*.

Nor is it even as easy as that.

The Police Procedural yarn-spinner has to know that a superintendent and a chief superintendent equate with a division . . . but, not always. That every force has spare supers and chief supers floating around; part of the 'establishment' but without clearly defined areas of clout.

He must know that chief constables, assistant chief constables, deputy chief constables and assistant deputy chief constables (and even deputy assistant chief constables) know their own power and authority, to the last heel click. They also know the other guy's power and authority. They are jealous of what they have, and have been known to screw things rotten in the sweet name of pettiness and personal aggrandisement.

He must also know that every rank, down to the humble pavement-crusher, has men who suffer from the same weakness. It is known as police politics and it, too, is part of a Police Procedural.

There are also unseen swings and unspoken balances which are necessary to make a force tick. Length of service, place of service and the personal experience of each officer adds tone-colour to opinions expressed and decisions made. And, however ephemeral, the author must catch these, also.

A small lifetime in a force can, of course, impart

this knowledge. It can also suffocate any natural gift of authorship. Stultifying officialese has the same effect as quick-drying cement on easy-flowing story-telling. 'He saw the woman and walked over' becomes 'he observed the female and proceeded towards her'.

Of the top ten in this sub-genre, only one (Wambaugh) is an ex-cop. The rest are 'policeman watchers' and have put what they've seen and heard to good use.

They also know the world of which they write – the police world – far better than any cop. The cop is part of that world, and much too near to notice. It is not at all like the non-police world. It is a more simple world and yet, at times, more involved. In the main, it is more tolerant but, in parts, it is much more maleficent.

All this becomes known to the author. Slowly, it is all understood. Then, if he knows his job – if he can think up a vehicle strong enough to hold, and carry, all these things – the knowledge becomes the stuff and sinews of a Police Procedural.

It has taken half a century and scores of fine word-smiths to reach this point; to rid the reading public of the gifted amateur who names the killer while the local law laces up its boots; to occasionally turn our back on the private eye, who fights a lonely, wise-cracking battle against impossible odds.

To gather courage enough – self-confidence enough – to suggest that even Chandler might sometimes be wrong.

He penned the best-known and most quoted essay in the history of crime writing. From his perch, above the rest, he prophesied that the crime novel had gone as far as it was capable of going; that it would go into decline and, in time, die.

It was a neat piece of self-promotion. In effect, he was saying, 'I'm good. Indeed, I'm more than good. I'm the best . . . now, and forever.'

Half of what he said was true. He was good . . . but not *that* good!

The ten names that top this category prove the point. In time they, too, will be elbowed aside. The sheer scan of the Police Procedural provides enough scope – has a wide enough horizon – and, at its best, it expands crime writing until the Crime Novel moves into the mainstream of great authorship.

Which is where it belongs.

John Wainwright is a prolific writer of police procedurals, based on his own experiences as a police officer.

PSYCHOLOGICAL SUSPENSE

LESLEY GRANT-ADAMSON

THE TOP TEN:

1. MALICE AFORETHOUGHT
Francis Iles (1931, 236 pages,
   Dent, £3.95 paperback)

2. A DARK ADAPTED EYE
Barbara Vine (1986, 300 pages,
   Penguin, £3.50 paperback)

3. STRANGERS ON THE TRAIN
Patricia Highsmith (1950, 256
   pages, Penguin, £3.50
   paperback)

4. JUDGEMENT IN STONE
Ruth Rendell (1977, 191 pages,
   Arrow, £3.50 paperback)

5. A KISS BEFORE DYING
Ira Levin (1953, 223 pages, Pan,
   £3.99 paperback)

6. THE TALENTED MR RIPLEY
Patricia Highsmith (1955, 249
   pages, Penguin, £3.50
   paperback)

7. BRIGHTON ROCK
Graham Greene (1938, 247
   pages, Penguin, £3.50
   paperback)

8. A DEMON IN MY VIEW
Ruth Rendell (1976, 184 pages,
   Arrow, £3.50 paperback)

9. BEAST IN VIEW
Margaret Millar (1955, 160
   pages, Penguin, £2.50
   paperback

10. THE COLLECTOR
John Fowles (1963, 277 pages,
   Pan, £3.99 paperback)

Labels are for jam; a novel is a blend too subtle for simple tagging. Yet publishers love them, reviewers fall for them. Only authors and readers stay unconvinced because reading and writing are arts of the subjective. Besides, it's a spell we're after, not a recipe.

A child who was asked to define the difference between a poem and a story decided that 'a story has more "and thens".' Quite so. And suspense fiction has the best "and thens". If not, the trick fails. Get it right, and the reader is beguiled, the characters floating tantalisingly in his mind during the periods he is forced to set the book aside and take care of real life.

'It's as though the people in the story are drawing me' is how this was described to me by a man who, well into his eighties, took to reading books. He turned away from Agatha Christie, when his third persuaded him they were predictable, and he found a different author better able to keep him dangling. The lady was Iris Murdoch, which says much about subjectivity when it comes to pinpointing suspense and much, too, about the capabilities of the uneducated reader faced with sophisticated novel-making.

When I've been obliged to choose my own favourite author in the genre, I've tussled each time with Simenon, Highsmith and Rendell/Vine. But always opted for Highsmith because of the spare, determined style that invests the mundane with menace. I'm fascinated that she can have me jittery over the page, biting my lip and thinking: 'Oh my God, this character's *making a cup of tea!*' Because of what we know about her cast and can hazard of their fate, every detail is imbued with excitement. Famously, Graham Greene remarked that she gives her reader a sense of personal danger. Less famously, one of my editors grumbled: 'Oh, she's so *slow*, nothing ever happens'; and a literary journalist despised her because her characters were sleazy and her backgrounds everyday.

Television has made people impatient with storytelling, fonder of glitz and glam. Viewers have come to expect rapid sure-fire scenes.

Establishing shot. Cut!

Character identification. Cut!

Plot development. Cut!

They are offered distracting scenery and settings, the emphasis frequently on style, and the story coming way down the priority list. Rerun those 1990 Eurotec series if you need to check this.

Meanwhile suspense novelists are doing it better. No nonsense about humanity's declining attention span, they conjure an emotion and they heighten and tighten until they wring the reader dry of it. No fuss, either, about elaborate settings and devilish means of murder – who needs a murder at all? Stir up sympathy for the hero, trap him in a predicament that causes the reader that inward gasp, and you're away.

Suspense fiction is a fine form for reader and writer to explore. Stimulating, because of the risk. No safety net of the tidy ending that's still, broadly, obligatory for the whodunnit. No guidelines or conventions except the need to work the spell. But when the author slips, the reader falls. I believe it takes a more accomplished novelist to write a superb suspense novel than any other kind of crime novel or, arguably, any other kind of novel. All round, it demands more. You can't get away with being weak on plot but having memorable characters. Or being a wizard with plot but hazy on theme.

Before I began to write I'd read little crime but fortunately I'd read well. I came across Highsmith in the Sixties,

Rendell in the next decade, plus P.D. James. That, leavened with Dick Francis, summed up my crime reading until I wrote a whodunnit rapidly followed by a suspense novel, and realised that part of the job was fielding questions from knowledgeable audiences and interviewers. They knew precisely where to stick the labels.

The most niggling question thrown at writers of suspense novels is the one that goes: 'Isn't it time you wrote a proper novel?', the inference being that suspense is close to mainstream fiction but substandard. I try to pin questioners down about this. Is the suspense novel less than the literary novel because

    a) it (sometimes) has lots of physical action?
    b) it (sometimes) deals with the nasty underside of society?
    c) it's (sometimes) written in the simplest style and language?

'Sometimes' keeps butting in because there are incontrovertible exceptions to every suggested rule. My clincher has been to ask back: 'What's substandard about *The Collector*?' Until now I assumed I was an oddity to be touting John Fowles' Booker Prize winner as one of the best suspense novels. The list unveiled in this book shows I was either jolly persuasive in argument or else, far likelier, most other people in the business thought so too.

Mention of the list means that I can prevaricate no longer. My guilty secret must be revealed. Whisper it if you will, but I don't like *Malice Aforethought*. It was favourite with thirty per cent more votes than the rest. Oh shame, I fell asleep during the first thirty pages, unthrilled by the tennis party or the girl rebuffing the doctor in the toolshed. More shame, I nodded off twice more before the finishing line. Suspecting I was being unfair, I reread. Well, I give up. I cannot like the book.

The other listed book that I hadn't read previously was Ira Levin's *A Kiss Before Dying*, and that has shot into my personal top ten. Although how can I dislodge a Celia Dale or a Margaret Yorke, for instance? But I mustn't tell you about Levin, Dale or Yorke; the brief is Francis Iles.

I canvassed members of the Crime Writers' Association for opinions kinder than mine and I shut them off immediately they digressed to the wonderful television adaptation with Hywel Bennet and a cast of. . . . No, no the *book*. Important, they said. Landmark, they said.

And so it is. Francis Iles was a pseudonym of Anthony Cox; born Watford 1893, died 1971; journalist and (as Iles) crime reviewer; founder member and first honorary secretary of the Detection Club; published 18 detective stories as Anthony Berkeley, three as Francis Iles, two as Anthony Cox, one play and three collections of journalism.

His first book, introducing Roger Sheringham, won praise for bringing a naturalistic quality to detective fiction. A later Berkeley story, *The Poisoned Chocolates Case*, delighted by lampooning detective fiction. In 1931 he used the Iles *nom de plume* for the book that became recognised as his masterpiece: *Malice Aforethought*. The first line reads: 'It was not until several weeks after he had decided to murder his wife that Dr Bickleigh took any active steps in the matter.' Sixty years on, that remains a brilliant line, containing the shock that a professional dedicated to doing good is plotting evil. In its day it was especially startling as the book is credited with being the first to tell the crime reader at the outset *what* happened and devote the other 200 or so pages to teasing him with details of *how* it happened.

Sound knowledge of police and legal procedure marked all of Berkeley/Iles' crime fiction, and perhaps it's unsurprising that I feel *Malice Aforethought* is strongest in the final third, after the inspector has called. The last chapter,

Thirteen and very unlucky for Dr Bickleigh, is a splendid piece of courtroom drama.

Iles understood that crime fiction was changing, and in *Malice Aforethought* he demonstrated one way it might be revitalised. He said: 'The detective story is in the process of developing into the crime novel . . . holding its readers less by mathematical than by psychological ties. The puzzle element will no doubt remain but it will remain of character rather than a puzzle of time, place, motive and opportunity.'

He was an innovator, a man on the lookout for improved ways of storytelling. I'm sorry I don't like his masterpiece better because I approve of crime writers who run risks, rip off the labels, and fashion new methods of saying "and then".

Lesley Grant-Adamson has written seven crime novels including three suspense novels, The Face of Death, Threatening Eye *and* Curse the Darkness. *Her other novels are* Patterns in the Dust, Guilty Knowledge, Wild Justice *and* Flynn. *All her books are published by Faber & Faber, in paperback too.*

THE WHODUNNIT

CATHERINE AIRD

THE TOP TEN

1. THE FRANCHISE AFFAIR
Josephine Tey (1948, 254
pages, Penguin, £3.99
paperback)

2. THE MOVING TOYSHOP
Edmund Crispin (1946, 205
pages, Penguin, £3.99
paperback)

3. PRESUMED INNOCENT
Scott Turow (1987, 423 pages,
Penguin, £4.99 paperback)

4. THE JOURNEYING BOY
Michael Innes (1949, 336 pages,
Penguin, £3.99 paperback)

5. A TASTE FOR DEATH
P.D. James (1986, 513 pages,
Penguin, £4.99 paperback)

6. PENNY BLACK
Susan Moody (1984, out of
print)

7. A RUNNING DUCK
Paula Gosling (1978, 202
pages, Pan, £2.50
paperback)

8. SMALLBONE DECEASED
Michael Gilbert (1950, 240
pages, Dent, £3.95
paperback)

9. THE SHORTEST WAY TO HADES
Sarah Caudwell (1984, 207
pages, Penguin, £2.99
paperback)

10. THE KILLINGS AT BADGER'S
DRIFT
Caroline Graham (1987, 264
pages, Headline, £2.99
paperback)

One day in February, 1753, a young domestic servant called Elizabeth Canning returned to her home after an unaccountable absence of a month from her place of employment. Fearful of the consequences, she spun a cock-and-bull story to her parents about having been abducted by a woman who then starved her in an upper room to compel her to live an immoral life; in which crime the woman had been aided and abetted by an old gypsy named Mary Squires.

Among the consequences (Elizabeth Canning was sentenced to seven years' transportation for perjury after one of the two women had been sentenced to hang and after the case had become the *cause célèbre* of the eighteenth century) was one that she could never have possibly imagined. It was that her story, most adroitly fictionalised and brought into the twentieth century, would head the list of whodunnits in this poll of crime writers as critics and readers.

Another mystery in its own right is how the author of *The Franchise Affair*, the playwright and crime novelist who used the name of Josephine Tey for this book, should have come to have written the story which over forty years after its publication has reached this position.

She was unmarried and had been educated in Inverness in Scotland and at – of all non-literary establishments – a Physical Education Training College. Apart from a brief foray into teaching, ended by the fatal illness of her mother, she spent almost her entire working life living at home with her widower father, whose infirmities increased with advancing age.

There are few people who would consider this a prescription for success, but any attempt to find a common denominator in the whodunnits which are listed is doomed to failure. On the contrary. Their very diversity serves to demonstrate the wide extent of writing covered within the genre of the detective story.

That this should now be more familiarly known as the whodunnit is in itself a tribute to the way in which this particular form of mystery writing has passed into the English language. The word was coined in 1930 by one Donald Gordon in the publication *American News of Books* and has certainly made up since for its late start, etymologically speaking.

Peer review is becoming a commonplace in medical circles in this country. When doctors, particularly surgeons, meet to consider the results they have obtained and the outcome of their treatment on their patients, it is not done, I understand, on the basis of 'didn't he do well' but rather 'could I have done better?' It is by no means common in the world of the crime writer and is an innovation to be welcomed.

The 'judgement of their peers' in this review has resulted in a series of much-loved titles coming to the fore. It is interesting to note that the books divide themselves into two quite distinct groups: those published round about the 1940s and those another forty years on, and that they exhibit a pronounced penchant for the amateur sleuth.

They are in the main themselves quite dateless and, considering that the proof of the literary pudding is usually in the eating (to mix a metaphor or two), it is noteworthy that they can be read and re-read with an enjoyment that does not depend entirely on the denouement. And nuggets of profundity can still found – like this in *The Journeying Boy* by Michael Innes:

'. . . although you can write poetry out of despair, just as you can write it out of joy, it's very hard to write it out of depression.'

One of the great joys of the genre itself is that there is room for pretty nearly everything within it. A study of these titles will show scenarios which range from a war-time operating theatre to present-day Washington, from a crusty solicitor's office to an improbably criminous Oxford. In writing detection there is room for the recondite: indeed, there is room for the very recondite.

However, although we 'have got a little list', it is important not to regard it as a complete conspectus of the whodunnit. There are works which are conspicuous by their absence. Some authors there be whose crime books fit in no one category – or in too many – for this form of psephological exercise.

A close study of those that are here will also show how the genre has moved on in a seemingly natural progression, first from the whodunnit to the howdunnit, and then, just as intriguingly, to the whydunnit. However nostalgically one harks back to a Golden Age, it is invigorating to have demonstrated 'before your very eyes' the fact that it is not a static field. Every Young Turk can, and does, have his or her day (perhaps in this connection the ancient legal phrase might be reversed and it be agreed that the female embraces the male) and no new development in science, law or moral turpitude has to wait long for its fictional chronicler.

That these chronicles are accurate, grammatical and faithfully reflect the social scene goes without saying; and yet it is this important contribution which is itself often unrecorded by those who come to study the specific period in which each particular whodunnit is set. Like it or

85

not, the writers of detective fiction, who of necessity are great attenders to detail, are, almost in passing, excellent observers of the society in which we live and about which they write.

Read them twice.

Catherine Aird has written some fourteen crime novels featuring Inspector Sloane. She is the current chairman of the Crime Writers' Association (1990–91).

HISTORY MYSTERY

PETER LOVESEY

THE TOP TEN

1. THE DAUGHTER OF TIME
Josephine Tey (1951, 191
    pages, Penguin, £3.99
    paperback)

2. THE NAME OF THE ROSE
Umberto Eco (1980, 502
    pages, Picador, £5.99
    paperback)

3. THE FALSE INSPECTOR DEW
Peter Lovesey (1982, 251
    pages, Arrow, £3.50
    paperback)

4. A MORBID TASTE FOR BONES
Ellis Peters (1977, 192
    pages, Futura, £2.99
    paperback)

5. THE LEPER OF ST. GILES
Ellis Peters (1981, 223
    pages, Futura, £3.50
    paperback)

6. THE DEVIL IN VELVET
John Dickson Carr (1951,
    out of print)

7. BERTIE AND THE TIN MEN
Peter Lovesey (1987, 230
    pages, Arrow, £2.50
    paperback)

8. DEATH COMES AS THE END
Agatha Christie (1945,
    219 pages, Fontana, £3.25
    paperback)

9. THE VIRGIN IN THE ICE
Ellis Peters (1982, 271
    pages, Futura, £3.50
    paperback)

10. THE WENCH IS DEAD
Colin Dexter (1989, 200
    pages, Pan, £3.99
    paperback)

Before he murdered his wife, the infamous Dr Crippen used to practise what he described as painless dentistry. In the same benevolent spirit I am about to outline a course of painless history. The idea may be of use to educationists. A passionate debate rages about the subject of history in the national curriculum. One camp argues for a basis of significant facts and dates; the other for an understanding of the conditions in which people lived. My proposal should satisfy everyone, and most of all the students. I have devised a history syllabus based totally on crime fiction.

The required reading begins with a curiosity piece from Agatha Christie, a story set in about 2000 B.C., *Death Comes as the End*. As one would expect from a writer who was the wife of an archaeologist, the Egypt of the Middle Kingdom is convincingly portrayed, and the plotting demonstrates that a good murder story has no need of Scotland Yard techniques for its resolution.

The ancient civilization of China, *circa* 670 A.D., is represented in the writing of Robert van Gulik, a distinguished Dutch diplomat who was an Oriental scholar. In 1940, van Gulik discovered and translated a seventeenth-century Chinese text, *Dee Goong An*, that became the inspiration for his Judge Dee novels and short stories featuring the cases of a magistrate who was a brilliant detective. Choosing one set book from the series is a difficult task, but *Necklace and Calabash* combines history, wit and detection most pleasingly.

For an entertaining way into early English history – or myth – I recommend *Our Man in Camelot*, by Anthony Price, a writer who demonstrates brilliantly in book after book that the past is often the key to learning about the present – which is surely the best justification for the study of history. Anyone who reads in Price's book the ingenious ways in which the CIA contrive to investigate King Arthur will be encouraged to absorb more history in *War Game*, about the Civil War, and other titles I shall mention later.

But we haven't left the Middle Ages yet. An indispensable source is the bestselling Brother Cadfael series by Ellis Peters, a marvellous evocation of monastic life in twelfth-century Shrewsbury. If I have a preference for the first Cadfael, *A Morbid Taste for Bones*, I must qualify it by saying that the series has maintained consistent excellence. The reader comes to know the Benedictine community intimately and it is impossible not to sense the common humanity that motivates the characters.

To give our brightest students a European perspective on monastic life, Umberto Eco's *The Name of the Rose* is the obvious choice. Set in Northern Italy two centuries later than the Cadfael books, it is an intricate series of puzzles, a demanding read with a strong philosophical content.

Now to a mediaeval mystery that still challenges interpretation. Did King Richard III order the murder of the boy princes in the Tower of London in 1483? Josephine Tey, in *The Daughter of Time*, gave a modern detective, her Inspector Grant, the task of investigating the story from his hospital bed. *The Daughter of Time* easily topped our crime writers' poll, earning nearly three times as many votes as the next choice. Although not all historians may agree with Inspector Grant's conclusion, the writing is persuasive and the book has actually been included in university reading lists. The proverbial 'daughter of Time' is truth; the underlying theme is the way in which truth is traduced down the ages to become bogus history, and if students are made aware that the so-called facts are not necessarily carved in stone, then they have learned something of more importance than the guilt or innocence of Richard III.

Josephine Tey's controversial conclusion spurred several other crime writers to investigate the fates of the princes.

The prolific American history/mystery writer, Elizabeth Peters, employed her librarian heroine to provide a different interpretation in *The Murders of Richard III*, while Guy Townsend, Jeremy Potter and Glenn Pierce have also built the story into crime novels.

John Dickson Carr had such a passion for history within the mystery form that he can span three centuries with novels of quality. *The Case of the Constant Suicides* brings two academics into conflict in 1940 over matters that happened during the reign of Charles II. Dickson Carr, a Cavalier at heart, had a special affection for the Restoration period. *The Devil in Velvet* is a swashbuckling mystery set mainly in 1675. With *The Demoniacs*, he switched to the mid-eighteenth century and the era of the Bow Street Runners. *Fire Burn!*, set in 1829, began a trilogy dedicated to the Metropolitan Police, and had among its characters the actual Commissioners at Scotland Yard, Richard Mayne and Charles Rowan. Another real individual, the famous Inspector Whicher, appeared in *Scandal at High Chimneys*, set in 1865, and *The Witch at Low Tide* brought the police into the Edwardian era with an 'impossible' crime in a bathing tent. The last novel Dickson Carr wrote, *The Hungry Goblin*, was set in London in 1869 and featured as his detective one of the pioneers of the genre, Wilkie Collins.

Since Wilkie Collins has come up, perhaps I should state here that my brief confines me to books written as history, rather than those which have acquired a period flavour since they were written. Thus *The Moonstone* and the Sherlock Holmes stories are covered elsewhere in this book (*see page 57*).

Let us return to the eighteenth century and *Dr Sam Johnson, Detector*. What the real Dr Johnson would have said about Lillian de la Torre's liberty in putting the great man to the solving of crime we can only conjecture. It is enough for the modern reader that the stories are scrupulously written, with wit and affection. In *Bloody Murder*, Julian Symons described them as 'perhaps the most successful pastiches in crime fiction.' Ms de la Torre has stated that it came to her in a flash of light that the only pair to equal the immortal Holmes and Watson were the immortal Johnson and Boswell.

Having referred to Dickson Carr's portrayal of the Bow Street Runners, I must not neglect to mention the novels of Jeremy Sturrock, narrated as if by the chief of the Bow Street Runners. Beginning in 1972 with *The Village of Rogues*, Sturrock established a strong, confident voice and a way of using his research unobtrusively. By an odd coincidence, in the same year that Sturrock's series was launched, Derek Lambert (writing as Richard Falkirk) published *Blackstone*, the first of several novels of action that featured another engaging Bow Street Runner, Edmund Blackstone.

It is understandable that the history taught in schools places a big emphasis on the nineteenth and twentieth centuries. Conveniently for my present task, the Victorian period is favoured more than any other by crime writers. Several better known for modern stories have published at least one Victorian mystery, among them Ed McBain (writing as Evan Hunter), Loren D. Estleman, H.R.F. Keating (as Evelyn Hervey), Gwendoline Butler and William Marshall. And there is a growing band of writers specialising in the period. Ray Harrison, Alanna Knight, Amy Myers and Anne Perry have each created a Victorian detective and a devoted readership.

My self-imposed challenge is to select a handful of titles to represent the Victorian era. Top of my list must be *Dear Laura* by Jean Stubbs. Reviewers often write of books as 'atmospheric'. I can think of none more atmospheric than this. Her Inspector Lintott is a credible policeman in a superbly told tale. *A Coffin for Pandora*, by Gwendoline Butler, is is another unforgettable Victorian mystery, in which a young governess is involved in a kidnapping and a murder. Colin Dexter's ingenious *The Wench is Dead*, with Inspector Morse investigating at a remove of 150 years, deservedly won the Gold Dagger of the Crime Writers' Association.

Of the several fine Victorian mysteries by Julian Symons, my choice is *Sweet Adelaide*, a retelling in the form of a novel of the tantalising true story of Adelaide Bartlett, accused of poisoning her husband. The book addresses itself to the plea raised after the trial: '. . . now that Mrs Bartlett has been found not guilty, she should tell us in the interests of science how she did it.'

At this stage my syllabus needs some light relief, so I turn to one of the Inspector Lestrade novels of M.J. Trow, *Lestrade and the Brother of Death*. Lestrade, originally a butt for Sherlock Holmes, deserves and seems to relish his independent existence in these resourceful and funny books.

Britain's imperial heyday is represented in my reading-list by *The Murder of the Maharajah*, by H.R.F. Keating, winner of the CWA Gold Dagger. Set in the Raj of 1930, it is a beautifully crafted whodunnit with a compelling sense of the time and place.

For the rest of history in the present century I can safely write: 'See the novels of Anthony Price, notably *Other Paths to Glory*, *The Hour of the Donkey*, *The '44 Vintage* and *Soldier No More*.' Military history and espionage are given an immediacy and a sense of involvement in Price's books that no textbook can supply.

There – the course is complete. Painless history. And compelling mystery.

Peter Lovesey has won both the Gold Dagger award (for The False Inspector Dew) *and the Silver Dagger award (for* Waxwork). *He is currently vice-chairman of the CWA (1990–91).*

ROMANTIC SUSPENSE

PAULA GOSLING

THE TOP TEN

1. GAUDY NIGHT
Dorothy L. Sayers (1935, 446
  pages, Coronet, £3.99
  paperback)

2. REBECCA
Daphne du Maurier (1938, 397
  pages, Pan, £3.99 paperback)

3. MY BROTHER MICHAEL
Mary Stewart (1960, 254 pages,
  Coronet, £2.99 paperback)

4. NINE COACHES WAITING
Mary Stewart (1958, 317 pages,
  Coronet, £3.99 paperback)

5. THE TAMARIND SEED
Evelyn Anthony (1971, 208
  pages, Sphere, £2.99
  paperback)

6. JANE EYRE
Charlotte Brontë (1847, 489
  pages, Penguin, £1.99
  paperback)

7. AIRS ABOVE THE GROUND
Mary Stewart (1965, 254
  pages, Coronet, £2.99
  paperback)

8. BRAT FARRAR
Josephine Tey (1949, 237
  pages, Penguin, £3.99
  paperback)

9. THE CIRCULAR STAIRCASE
Mary Roberts Rinehart (1909,
  182 pages, Dent, £3.95
  paperback)

10. NIGHT WITHOUT STARS
Winston Graham (out of
  print)

Some attribute the origin of the Romantic Suspense novel to Mrs Radcliffe, who wrote *The Castle of Otranto*, and make much of 'Gothic' origins. I would agree – if setting were the only criterion. But novels of Romantic Suspense are not all built around cobwebbed castles and ghostly footsteps, nor do they require Exotic Locales, Horrid Villains, or Secret Rooms and Staircases, although any and all of these constituents may be included.

According to the dictionary, 'romance' involves passion, grandeur and imagination. Not all passions require a clinch, and indeed, passion may not concern human love at all, but exhibit itself in loyalty to a country or an obsession to possess an object or a wild determination to survive.

As far as suspense goes, we might be on similarly equivocal ground, as many novels in this category are told in the first-person, somewhat attenuating suspense by the obvious survival of the central character to tell the tale.

So if these things – exotic locale, romancing, and suspense – were all, we could include novels by Alastair Maclean and Desmond Bagley in the category of Romantic Suspense. But we do not – so there must be something more.

In fact, there are two things more.

Firstly – *the protagonist*. A Romantic Suspense novel almost invariably centres around a young woman. That is not to say the central character couldn't be a man, nor that all crime novels with female protagonists are Romantic Suspense. But the protagonist in a novel of Romantic Suspense must have certain motivations – goals not usually the concern of Sherlock Holmes or Hercule Poirot. Male 'detectives' are generally motivated by a search for Truth. The protagonist of a Romantic Suspense novel, on the other hand, is motivated by a search for Happiness.

Secondly – *the central mystery*. Crime novels concern a specific crime – usually murder – and chart the process of solving that crime. Romantic suspense novels are concerned with solving *situations*. They chart the progress of the heroine through an atmosphere of conflicting emotions and confusing activity as she attempts to understand the situation she is in, and ultimately to find happiness and peace. That is why, for her, the central mystery is *the hero himself*, because he is both antagonist and prize.

By those criteria, the real begetter of Romantic Suspense is not Mrs Radcliffe, but Charlotte Brontë, with her novel *Jane Eyre*. Here we find the sympathetic heroine with her travails, hopes and dreams, and, towering over everything that happens, the enigmatic and sublimely fascinating mystery of Mr Rochester himself. Instinctively she knows that if she understands him, she will understand All.

That pattern continues from then until now, without basic change. Whether hanging from a cliff edge, or being pursued by bears, or stalked by a mad axeman, or trapped by rising waters – the heroine of a good novel of Romantic Suspense is still generally preoccupied by what on earth Jeremy, David, Scott, Brand, Adam, Tony or Brett are *really* like.

If a novel of Romantic Suspense is the story of one woman's struggle against inimical forces, both physical and emotional, and her eventual triumph over them, then her reward is usually – but not always – the love of the hero.

Of course, it is easy to find humour in all this – phrases like 'damsel in distress' roll easily off the scoffer's tongue – and the wry description 'girl gets house' is often justified, for many novels in this category include the winning of riches and social prestige along with the love of the hero. (Perhaps the days of seeking simple joy in the arms of a

95

noble artisan are gone – after all, look what happened when woman stooped to gamekeeper!)

Certainly crime and romance are the most-sold and most-read categories of all fiction, and therefore are more vulnerable to exploitation by both second-rate authors and greedy publishers. Antagonism or derision are deserved and justified when dealing with poorly-written novels of *any* description. But just as it is difficult to reduce *Crime and Punishment* to 'Boy Kills Old Lady, Feels Rotten, and Gets Just Deserts', so it is equally difficult to reduce a novel like *Jane Eyre* to 'Poor Girl Gets Above Herself But Wins Through In The End'.

It is all in the telling, after all.

But why combine Romance and Suspense, anyway?

I think it has to do with vulnerability.

When we turn to crime fiction of any description, it is with the confidence that, in the end, All Will Be Well. What fascinates is how this end will be achieved. If the detective is as intelligent as Sherlock Holmes, it will be by scientific and intellectual means. If he is as bold and resourceful as James Bond, it will be by brute force and a big gun. If he is as wily and street-smart as Lew Archer, it will be by observation and cunning. And if he is a member of – say – the 87th Precinct, it will be by teamwork and persistence. In all these things, as noted earlier, it is Truth that is the goal.

But a vulnerable protagonist raises doubts as to how peace will be achieved. Our Girl does not carry a cigarette lighter that fires anaesthetic darts, she does not have five hundred uniformed men at her beck and call, she may be bright but does not possess the frontal-lobe development of the Holmes brothers, and while she may prove brave, it could well be the kind of misplaced bravery that leads her into far deeper waters than any cautious man would attempt. After all, it is her heart, not her head, that is leading her on. In novels of Romantic Suspense, therefore, it is a truism that however bad the situation is, the vulnerability of the heroine *will make it worse*, not better. We will therefore be more worried about her and ultimately more relieved and satisfied at the end.

In the earlier days, we had heroines who were prone to faint. We also had narrators who fell into what Ogden Nash called the 'Had I But Known' or HIBK girls, a group that turned foreshadowing into whine art. But heroines of modern Romantic Suspense have moved on. Even if they are placed in an historical context, they are generally braver and more resourceful than those wilting women who carried smelling salts at all times because they knew that, given a challenge, collapse was the only ladylike alternative. One wonders why they thought a prone position was protective – but then, the past *is* another country, they undid things differently there.

If one were to assess the category of Romantic Suspense as a whole, I think it would fairly break down into two halves – Historic and Modern – divided by time rather than type, setting rather than content. The heroine in an historic setting is limited by the conventions of her times as to her actions and responses, and unenlightened by psychological insights that would be second nature to a post-Freudian protagonist. Her dangers are therefore all the more intimidating, and certainly her vulnerability is greater. It could be argued that such books are thus more exciting and ultimately more satisfying, *because* they do not contain easy answers – such as picking up the telephone and screaming for help. The massive sales for these books would certainly indicate that our appetite for historic predicament remains as yet unappeased.

In point of fact, modern settings for romantic suspense make things much more difficult for the writer. If the heroine *can* pick up the telephone, or pack a .22 in her handbag, where is the threat to her survival?

In complexity.

More and more frequently today, good novels in this category contain added considerations that blur the edges of the definition itself. There might be a corpse, there might be a serious crime, there might even be elements of espionage and technology. In the pursuit of these side-lines – for while they add excitement and texture they *are* sidelines – the heroine as modern woman *copes*. Because today's heroines *are* a different breed, they also possess distinct advantages over male detectives. Being women, and therefore far better equipped than a mere male to notice and attend to detail, the heroine of a modern novel of Romantic Suspense may well discover Truth and precipitate Justice along her way. But any triumphs of detection or espionage she achieves will not diminish her real intent, which is still to bring order out of chaos. This is, traditionally and reluctantly, a female role. We may not all like it (so much of it seems to involve spring cleaning), but it is one for which we have a definite and proven ability.

Now, an equally traditional role for the professional critic has been to deem and damn novels of Romantic Suspense as 'trivial'. But the intent to re-establish order is hardly a trivial undertaking when the situation is both dire and complicated. And the creation of a believeable heroine motivated by such an intent – either consciously or subconsciously – is no small matter for a writer.

To put a badge on a detective is the work of but a moment – it can be an official gold shield in a wallet, or an arbitrary number such as 007, or the implied badge of the Gifted Amateur With a History of Success in Similar Enquiries – but the badge gives him instant authority in the reader's eyes. He doesn't have to be real or realistic –

he simply has to be labelled – and you will listen to what he has to say.

But a woman caught up in a web of deceit, confusion, cross-purposes, shadows, memories, whispers, half-heard phrases and haunting dreams has no badge. In order to be listened to she has to be appealing, she has to be honourable, she has to be persistent, and, above all, she has to be *interesting*.

The requirement of believeable central characters is basic to all good novels, of course. But Romantic Suspense deals with feelings rather than fingerprints, bloodstains, and train schedules, and feelings are notoriously difficult to write about. Throwing in a handful of exclamation marks is *not* enough.

Daphne Du Maurier, whose novel *Rebecca* is the consistent first choice among writers and readers of Romantic Suspense, stood firmly behind her declaration that *Rebecca* was not a crime novel – although there is a crime; nor a novel of place – although the setting of Manderley is both splendid and haunting: nor a novel of psychopathy – although, heaven knows, the undercurrents of aberrant behaviour are strong in it. No, she said, *Rebecca* is 'a study in jealousy'.

So it is. But it fulfils all the criteria of Romantic Suspense in the most masterful way – a heroine who is innocent yet full of subtle possibilities, caught up in a situation that is both contradictory and intimidating, whose consuming interest is to discover the true feelings and bring about the happiness of the mysteriously tortured hero, Maxim de Winter. Above all, it is beautifully written, by an author who wore no critic's genre label.

It should thus come as no surprise that most of the truly outstanding authors of Romantic Suspense are authors who are well-respected in other fields. Mary Stewart is a university lecturer. 'Victoria Holt' is but one of the pseudonyms of the noted historic novelist Jean Plaidy. Phyllis Whitney has been both editor and teacher. The earlier American proponents of the art of combining romance and mystery, such as Mary Roberts Rinehart and Mignon B. Eberhardt, have been followed by writers such as Ursula Curtiss and Mary McMullen – sisters, by the way – who, through their own experiences in the world of commerce, have brought the bright world of the career girl into the equation.

Through these, and many others, the genre of Romantic Suspense has grown and continues to grow. As does the skill and the imagination of those who write it. Somewhere, someone is writing another *Rebecca*, another *Jane Eyre*.

Millions of readers await.

Paula Gosling was the winner of the John Creasey Award in 1978 (for A Running Duck *– which was made into the film* Cobra, *starring Sylvester Stallone) and the CWA Gold Dagger in 1985 (for* Monkey Puzzle*). She has produced nine crime novels and was chairman of the CWA 1988–89.*

THRILLERS

TIM HEALD

THE TOP TEN:

1. ROGUE MALE
Geoffrey Household (1939, 192 pages, Penguin, £2.99 paperback)

2. THE DAY OF THE JACKAL
Frederick Forsyth (1971, 412 pages, Corgi, £3.99 paperback)

3. THE MASK OF DIMITRIOS
Eric Ambler (1939, 268 pages, Fontana, £2.95 paperback)

4. THE EAGLE HAS LANDED
Jack Higgins (1975, 383 pages, Pan, £3.99 paperback)

5. THE DANGER
Dick Francis (1983, 286 pages, Pan, £3.99 paperback)

6. THE ROSE OF TIBET
Lionel Davidson (1962, out of print)

7. TWICE SHY
Dick Francis (1981, 269 pages, Pan, £3.50 paperback)

8. GORKY PARK
Martin Cruz Smith (1981, 335 pages, Pan, £3.99 paperback)

9. THE SUN CHEMIST
Lionel Davidson (1976, out of print)

10. THE GUNS OF NAVARONE
Alistair Maclean (1957, 255 pages, Fontana £2.50 paperback)

For six years (1983–1989) I was the 'Thriller' reviewer of *The Times*. True to the traditions of the paper I duly thundered out every month or so, pontificating on the virtues of an extraordinary number of very fat books, most of them – it seemed to me – with hammers and sickles, Union Jacks, swastikas or stars and stripes on the cover. Oh, those fifth-hand descriptions of the Oval Office in the White House, those Moscow street plans based on the Intourist A-to-Z. Ah, those macho men with their incessant 'shooty-bangs' (John le Carre's laconic put-down phrase) and those inevitable available ladies with their 'generous mouths', 'high cheek-bones' and 'pert breasts'. In the end I couldn't bear another airport lounge or AK-47 and I gave up. It was, it seemed to me, a sub-genre that had had its day. The thriller wasn't thrilling any more.

The sub-division into 'Crime', reviewed by the estimable Marcel Berlins, and 'Thrillers' was instituted after the departure of H.R.F. Keating who had managed, with characteristic urbanity, to review both. I was never quite sure how the literary editor, who took a perverse pleasure in knowing nothing whatever about either, distinguished between them. I think he simply sent Marcel the thin books and gave me the fat ones. Maybe he sampled them briefly and assigned anything with a vicar or a spinster to my colleague while sending me the ones which had characters called Ivan, Tatiana, Nathan or Kate.

Part of my disillusion was having yardsticks that set standards which, if one is being fair, are almost impossible to emulate. One of them, I'm delighted to say, is the book which came top of the CWA poll. I first heard *Rogue Male* read out loud to me by Randall Hoyle, headmaster of my prep school, who had the laudable and educative habit of reading aloud to the school every Sunday evening after prayers. His choice of subject was, I suppose, mainstream. He was heavy on the Conan Doyle historicals;

Moonfleet; John Buchan; Rider Haggard. The qualities were those which became, for me, the ultimate accolade, when reviewing books for *The Times*. If I really liked it I would conclude, not alpha plus, but 'rattling good yarn.'

No yarn is more rattlingly good than *Rogue Male*. For sheer pace and excitement it is unmatchable. First published in 1939, it had an initial edge of startling topicality. Upper-class Englishman attempts to kill mad-dog Führer. What, as the storm clouds gathered and Hitler's forces ate into free Europe, could be more apposite? Every Englishman worth his salt would have given his all for a crack at the Führer. Sir Robert Hunter is Everyman's 'Me'; the foul dictator is a universal 'Them'.

But then, of course, he doesn't succeed. And gallant failure for an English audience is so infinitely more seductive than cheap success. We do so love a loser and Hunter is a two-time loser. First he is taken by the dictator's men, tortured and interrogated. Then, back home, he finds no help from his own people. He goes, literally, to earth. These are the scenes, in Hardy's own beautiful county of Dorset, which most of us, I think, remember. The return of the native is an absolute return in which he lives like a wild animal, pitting his wits against an unknown enemy who is immeasurably more powerful and well equipped than he himself. This is one man against the world; the individual against the soulless state; David against Goliath. The setting is an English countryside that we all know and love and in which, instinctively, we feel safe. But here . . .

This 'contra mundum' feel of the brave individual battling away against insuperable odds is the core of many of the best novels in the genre. Even *Rogue Male*, brilliant and original though it is, owes something, whether consciously or not, to a number of predecessors. The very concept of 'hero' suggests the notion of a lone individual

103

against the world and it is one of the oldest basic plots in the whole of literature.

It is there also in John Buchan's *The Thirty Nine Steps*, the quintessential 'chase' novel published just after the outbreak of World War One. Same basic theme: filthy foreign fiends against a stiff upper-lipped Englishman (though Buchan's Richard Hannay was South African). It helps the plot, though not the hero, that the enemy has an amorphous blob-like quality. Shades of Kafka. We don't know who it is, who they are. The smiling ticket collector, the friendly hotel receptionist, the available blonde . . . they too could be the enemy . . . Careless Talk Costs Lives. *The Thirty-Nine Steps* features in another list but it also belongs here and it too had a huge following from the voters.

It's no coincidence, I think, that the biggest votes in this genre were recorded for books that have this element of one against many. The dinosaur-crunching of power block against power block only comes in further down the scale and even then is alleviated by the sense of the essential protagonists being cogs within the wheels. We can't identify with the CIA or the KGB. We need individuals within them to make them real.

Not that we need, in these days, at least, to have a true hero to identify with. *Never Come Back* by John Mair, much championed by Julian Symons, Dilys Powell and, scandalously, not in these lists, has a real anti-hero as its protagonist. Recently televised, it, like *Rogue Male* is an anti-fascist tract. Entertainment is never 'just entertainment'. There is a message in all good books. Forsyth's *Day of the Jackal* is an anti-hero book. The Jackal is a rat. Not only that, he is intent on committing a crime, the assassination of de Gaulle, which we know never succeeded. It is one of the many brilliances of this book that Forsyth makes us believe that perhaps history is wrong and he is right.

I have no real quarrel with the votes of my colleagues but they excite comment, and a certain amount of grumbling. It is interesting at least that Cruz Smith's *Gorky Park* scores so high but that he as an author does less well. Conversely, where are Gavin Lyall and Anthony Price? Both scored points but there was no concordat about a particular book. Like Dick Francis, the only man to score twice in the top ten, they are respected for a body of work rather than an individual book. I think nearly all Dick Francis books are brilliant yet I can't tell one from another. They are a seamless tapestry.

I dare say Deighton and le Carré, packed with action and thrills, surface in some other part of the park. The women too. Though why so few? I can only think of Helen McInnes (excellent), Evelyn Anthony and Dorothy Dunnett. Why do women detect but seldom thrill? Another area for discussion.

The inclusions speak, more or less, for themselves. I have some extra thoughts. Do crime writers distrust the sea? *HMS Ulysses* is more thrilling than *The Guns of Navarone*. Hammond Innes is more thrilling than almost anyone. Likewise Nicholas Monsarrat. Where is Gerald Seymour? And Tim Sebastian? What about Ken Follett and good old Desmond Bagley? Am I alone in thinking *The Manchurian Candidate* one of the all time great action thrillers? Has no-one else heard of Brian Cleeve?

But one could go on like this for ever. The English, as this list demonstrates, are among the world's great yarn-spinners. We, especially the blokes, tell a bloody good action-packed story. Beginning, middle and end (happy). Good guy. Bad guys. Beautiful girl (who hero gets). That's the first division. But please God preserve us from those who follow in their steps. The best thrillers are not only more thrilling than any other book alive but also intellectually satisfying. The greatest writers in the world have not shied away from action and thrill: *War and Peace, A Tale of Two Cities, Lord Jim*. But the second division in this field is truly second-rate. God save us all from the imitations.

They may flatter but they certainly don't deceive.

Tim Heald has created the Simon Bognor series, as well as producing journalism for a number of different newspapers and books on specialist subjects ranging from cricket to the Royal Family. He was chairman of the CWA 1987–88.

ESPIONAGE FICTION

JAMES MELVILLE

THE TOP TEN

1. THE SPY WHO CAME IN
   FROM THE COLD
   John le Carré (1963, 220 pages,
   Coronet, £3.50 paperback)

2. THE IPCRESS FILE
   Len Deighton (1962, 272 pages,
   Grafton, £2.95 paperback)

3. TINKER, TAILOR, SOLDIER, SPY
   John le Carré (1974, 367 pages,
   Coronet, £4.50 paperback)

4. FROM RUSSIA WITH LOVE
   Ian Fleming (1957, 208 pages,
   Coronet, £2.50 paperback)

5. GAME, SET AND MATCH
   Len Deighton (*Berlin Game*:
   1983, 325 pages, Grafton, £3.50
   paperback; *Mexico Set*: 1984,
   381 pages, Grafton, £3.50
   paperback; *London Match*:
   1985, 405 pages, Grafton,
   £3.50 paperback)

6. THE THIRD MAN
   Graham Greene (1950, 157
   pages, Penguin, £2.99
   paperback)

7. THE LABYRINTH MAKERS
   Anthony Price (1974, 239
   pages, Grafton, £2.95
   paperback)

8. THE QUILLER MEMORANDUM
   Adam Hall (1965, out of print)

9. THE RIDDLE OF THE SANDS
   Erskine Childers (1903, 268
   pages, Dent, £3.50
   paperback)

10. THE KEY TO REBECCA
    Ken Follett (1980, 341 pages,
    Corgi, £2.99 paperback)

'Without some dissimulation no business can be carried on at all', as Lord Chesterfield pointed out in a letter to his son. That is indeed a law of nature. Plants practise it, and so do insects, birds, sea creatures and terrestrial animals, including of course ourselves. Some competence in the use of the arts of deception is essential to the survival on this earth of every living species.

It ill becomes that notorious bungler the human being in particular to claim any special ingenuity in this context. However, it is obvious that even the most basic business of scratching some sort of subsistence is likely to involve simple dissimulation of some kind. Hunters and gatherers need camouflage, tillers of the soil construct scarecrows, and so on. Moreover, a minority of members of the human race do, unlike other adult animals, have time and energy to spare, with which they have always sought to promote or protect their interests in a variety of more sophisticated ways.

Curiosity is also a natural instinct and one to be cultivated as an essential aid to physical survival; and, as in the case of deceit, it manifests itself in refined forms once the basic necessities of life are secured. Spying is one such form of applied curiosity, and is an everyday activity for many.

Some snoop for a living, acting as informers. Others, who can afford to do it vicariously, by employing others to spy on their behalf. Yet others go in for spying just for the fun of it. We may well include many writers of espionage stories in this category, for perhaps the most elaborate way both to indulge and to profit from our fascination with secrets is to invent and make up stories about people who deal in them. Even if only by swapping gossip, we all traffic in confidential information some of the time, and readers in their millions have shown that they enjoy descriptions of the experiences of fictional characters who do it in demanding circumstances and in some style.

To possess information not generally available to others is to be in a position to exercise power: perhaps political, perhaps economic, perhaps psychological. Children learn about the last kind the first time they hear somebody chanting 'I've got a secret!' in the playground; and exercise it when they follow suit. No matter that the 'secret' referred to is usually banal or absurd: to be denied access to it makes others not only very cross but also a bit uneasy. Storytellers from the earliest times have exploited this fact of life; and most fiction involves elements of concealment, deception and discovery.

Secrets, particularly official secrets, are however the very stuff of espionage stories as currently defined by publishers, booksellers and librarians. As an identifiable genre, such fiction is a twentieth-century phenomenon which enjoyed a remarkable flowering in the postwar decades, and is now possibly on the decline. It comprises stories about secret agents of one kind or another, operating mostly within the context of international political intrigue.

A twentieth-century phenomenon? It might be objected that, even considering books in English only, the popular fiction of the nineteenth century was also well provided with examples of both professional and amateur 'political' spies. What about *The Scarlet Pimpernel*, *The Prisoner of Zenda* and the rest? What about Sherlock Holmes and the keen practical interest he took in the recovery of the stolen Bruce-Partington submarine plans, not to mention the hush-hush nature of the duties of his brother Mycroft, and Sherlock's collection of tokens of gratitude for confidential services rendered from his own Sovereign and various lesser but still eminent political personages? Don't they count?

Well, no, not really; and nor for that matter do James

Bond and the host of Bond derivatives who populate the sub-genre of tongue-in-cheek, deliberately over-the-top spoof spy books. In spite of this, *From Russia With Love* has a place in our list. The wacky original-ity and compulsive readability of Ian Fleming's *oeuvre* could not be ignored, any more than Graham Greene's splendid entertainment *Our Man In Havana* (the plot of which however does strike the reader as being as deliciously possible as it is hilarious). Nevertheless these and countless others of the same general type are fun books, not novels in the best sense of the word.

The essential point about 'proper' espionage fiction (including Greene's *The Third Man*, also in our list) on the other hand is that on the whole it purports to deal not in make-believe but in truths; aspiring to a combination of gritty realism, credibility in characterisation and back-ground authenticity. Though in quality it cannot begin to compare with the work of contemporary masters, it is fitting that the earliest book to have won a place in our list of top ten spy stories should be *The Riddle Of The Sands* by Erskine Childers.

The story of Childers' own career sounds like something dreamed up by an aspiring thriller writer. A product of Haileybury and Cambridge, he served as a House of Com-mons clerk for fifteen years, and as an Honourable Artillery Company volunteer took part in the Boer War. Childers enjoyed messing about in boats, exploring the coastlines of Britain and her nearer neighbours. His landmark novel came out in 1903, and certainly carried conviction. So much so that it was instrumental in alerting the government of the day to Britain's lack of coastal defences and consequent vulnerability to seaborne invasion. A dozen or so years later, Childers had become a Lieutenant Commander in the Royal Navy and been awarded the DSC. A fitting recognition of his patriotic zeal, one might think, until informed that Childers ended his life before a British firing squad as a member of the IRA.

It was however the emergence of organised, covert intelligence services as instruments of national government that gave birth to the espionage novel as we know it today: something very different from the romantic thriller or adventure story of earlier times. As what many writers quaintly refer to as the 'intelligence community' swelled in reality into a monstrous international bureaucracy, so novelists (many of them British and a number of these having been formally or informally employed in intelligence work) found it to be a rich, seemingly inexhaustible source of material.

They began to think more or less seriously about spies. For previous generations of writers, such people were, if low-grade, merely contemptible, venal informers. If high-grade and of the story-teller's own nationality, they were noble, intrepid patriots; if on the other side, sinister arch-villains. It was high time for something subtler; and as portrayed by the best in the field, the spy as career bureaucrat and oftentimes anti-hero proved for some decades to be a bestseller.

Not that the good old war-horse themes of patriotism and treachery were neglected. Far from it. Popular fiction must reflect topics of interest to those to whom it is sold, and the postwar decades were marked by scandal after scandal involving real-life spies, often persons in high places. People read in their newspapers about individuals who acted in the interests of foreign powers for reasons of ideological commitment. They read about others who did so because they had been bought or were being blackmailed; they read about defectors and moles, double agents and ingenious techniques and gadgets, and some at least were startled to discover that in times of theoretical peace ostensibly moral, God-fearing senior

111

officials serving democratically elected governments are authorised to instruct their subordinates to commit all manner of criminal acts in the name of political expediency.

The writers of much pot-boiling postwar espionage fiction simply made use of such revelations, embroidering them to a greater or lesser extent and populating their stories with characters obtained from Central Casting. They fed the chauvinism of readers by suggesting that the cloak-and-dagger boys and girls on 'our' side are not only braver, tougher, cleverer, more resourceful, nicer and sexually more successful than their opponents; but that unlike the said opponents, when they kill people it is with a certain regret, or at least with a witty, apposite comment on their lips.

The achievements of the truly original writers on our list are of a completely different kind. It is unnecessary to labour the obvious by dwelling on the fact that they tell good stories: they wouldn't have become bestsellers if they didn't. Their fellow writers pay homage to them not only because of their mastery of the form and their technical skills as novelists. Above all they are admired because they have convinced us and tens of millions of readers that intelligence work, even at the sharp end, is in fact mostly carried out by ordinary, flawed, frail and touchy human beings who have to be trained, managed, humoured, rewarded, disciplined and all the rest of it by senior civil servants often preoccupied with their own promotion prospects or personal problems.

Oddly enough these fine novels about spies commonly have precious little about actual spying in them. References to the setting up of networks in the field and accounts of the insertion of agents in and their extraction from hostile territory abound; but we are seldom told what they got up to while at work. Modern equivalents of the Bruce-Partington submarine plans figure hardly at all.

112

Battles are mostly of wits. The elaborate traps that are set are mostly psychological, and the protagonists often have as much or more to fear from the intrigues and real or imagined treachery of their colleagues and superiors than they do from their ostensible opponents (whom they tend to hold in some esteem and even occasionally affection, and every so often take out to lunch). Office politics count for more than the ideological struggle; and the manoeuvring involved in setting up a covert meeting are described much more explicity than the matters to be discussed.

John le Carrés *The Spy Who Came In From The Cold* is acclaimed as the number one by the overwhelming majority of the crime and thriller writers who took part in this exercise. Published in 1963, it was le Carré's third novel (and incidentally also the third in which the character of Smiley figured). It was deservedly a smash hit, and has had enormous influence on the work of a whole generation of espionage writers.

Known to have been involved for some years in intelligence work, le Carré describes its minutiae with an assurance and air of authority which hardly ever manifests itself as objectionable knowingness. He has often stressed that many of the appealing technical terms used in his books (lamp-lighter, baby-sitter, tradecraft etc.) are pure inventions, but one suspects that by now they have passed into the jargon of the real-life professionals. The jargon, and indeed the whole beautifully realised background, is nevertheless not what the book is really about.

For le Carré, the proper study of mankind is man. His themes are broad and significant, his characters painfully credible and the dilemmas confronting them of a kind most people can recognise as humanly important. Le Carré wrestles with the fundamental ethical problems usually ignored by those who treat espionage as a kind of game devised and played mainly by overgrown schoolboys, and truly illuminates the human condition.

Few will question his status as the master.

James Melville spent many years working abroad as a cultural diplomat. The time he spent in this capacity in Japan is reflected in his crime series featuring Superintendent Otani of the Hyogo prefectural police force. He is currently on the committe of the Crime Writers' Association.

HARDBOILED

REGINALD HILL

THE TOP TEN:

1. THE BIG SLEEP
Raymond Chandler (1939, 220 pages, Penguin, £4.50 paperback)

2. FAREWELL MY LOVELY
Raymond Chandler (1940, 254 pages, Penguin, £4.50 paperback)

3. THE MALTESE FALCON
Dashiell Hammett (1930, 201 pages, Pan, £3.50 paperback)

4. THE LONG GOODBYE
Raymond Chandler (1953, 320 pages, Penguin £4.99 paperback)

5. THE POSTMAN ALWAYS RINGS TWICE
James M. Cain (1934, included in *The Five Great Novels of James M. Cain*, 633 pages, Picador, £5.95 paperback)

6. THE GLASS KEY
Dashiell Hammet (1931, 220 pages, Pan, £1.95 paperback)

7. THE LADY IN THE LAKE
Raymond Chandler (1943, 238 pages, Penguin, £4.99 paperback)

8. RED HARVEST
Dashiell Hammett (1929, included in *The Four Great Novels*, 784 pages, Picador, £7.99 paperback)

9. THE GLASS HIGHWAY
Loren Estleman (1984, 179 pages, Papermac, £3.95 paperback)

10.= FREAKY DEAKY
Elmore Leonard (1988, 341 pages, Penguin, £3.99 paperback)

10.= OUTLAWS
George V Higgins (1987, 360 pages, Abacus, £3.99 paperback)

10=. THE GODWULF MANUSCRIPT Robert B. Parker (1974, 175 pages, Penguin, £2.99 pages)

So, what is hardboiled?

Well, it's been on the heat a lot longer than softboiled. And it isn't served in a china cup at a country house breakfast but out of a chipped bowl on the free lunch counter of some sleazy waterfront dive. And you don't open it with a crested silver spoon, you crack it against a scarred mahogany bar, peel the shell into an overcrowded ashtray, and float it down whole on a rip-tide of bourbon.

Historians have traced its origins back to the dime novels of the last century but all we really need to know is that its distinctive elements of style and content first manifested themselves beyond dispute in *Black Mask*, founded in 1920 as just another of H.L. Mencken's pulp magazines, but which under a succession of creative editors radically reshaped the detective story. Here is where anyone seriously interested in hardboiled has to start, for it is here that Dashiell Hammett's tales of the fat, unnamed, cynically streetwise Continental Op first appeared.

It's conventional, which means convenient, to say that Hammett invented hardboiled, but it's not strictly true. Some critics point to Carrol John Daly's 1922 story *The False Burton Combs* as the first true example of the genre, others give the credit to the *Black Mask* editors who encouraged and nurtured it. But the truth lies in history itself, which in the space of a century and a half had rushed America from the morning joys of liberty, fraternity and equality, through a high noon of wealth and power, into the twilight of economic depression, organised crime and civic corruption. Hardboiled didn't need to be invented; it came as naturally to this society as leaves to the tree.

What Hammett certainly did was legitimise it by taking it out of pulp and putting it on coated paper between hardcovers with the publication in 1929 of *Red Harvest*, the first version of which had appeared in four episodes in *Black Mask*. This, like *The Dain Curse* which followed

116

the same year, is a Continental Op story. The language is direct, the idiom vernacular, the action fast and violent, and the Op who tells the story, though his own morality is sometimes dubious, is clearly the agent of morality.

The two novels that follow, *The Maltese Falcon* and *The Glass Key*, are Hammett's masterworks, and it's no surprise to see them in the CWA list, though it's arguable that but for the cult status of the Bogart film, my distinguished colleagues might have reversed their order. In them Hammett has moved away from the first person narrative, which was to become almost a cliché of the hardboiled school, to third person, giving himself a wider range of options without abandoning the unifying tone of telling the story from the viewpoint of his still ambiguous heroes, Sam Spade and Nick Beaumont. He reverted to first person for his last completed book, *The Thin Man*, in which, by elevating the wise-cracking humour of hardboiled to a higher plane, he produced perhaps the finest comedy of detective manners.

While Hammett may not have invented the style, he explored its possibilities in every direction to such devastating effect that it was almost impossible for any subsequent hardboiled writer to find his or her own voice without passing through a period of Hammett pastiche.

Raymond Chandler acknowledges the debt generously, though he clearly regards himself as standing on Hammett's shoulders rather than sitting at his feet. However you vote in that debate – and the majority of CWA members are clearly Chandlerites – I find it strange that they should have put *The Big Sleep* ahead of *Farewell My Lovely* and especially *The Long Goodbye*.

The Big Sleep is very unevenly written. There are scenes which are all right, but there are other scenes which are far too pulpy. And he sure did run the similes into the ground! (Anyone inclined to howl in protest should note that the last three sentences are Chandler's, not mine. Perhaps Bogart influenced the vote once more?)

Nevertheless, despite its flaws, this complicated tale of the rotten rich Sternwood family, 'cannibalised' (Chandler's word) from a couple of his *Black Mask* stories, is a splendid manifesto of his artistic ends and sampler of his artistic means. In it he declares open war on the corruption of wealth, introduces us to the often imitated but never excelled cynical/sentimental, streetwise/chivalrous, realist/romantic persona of Philip Marlowe, creates a marvellous sense of place, and above all writes with a richness which at its best gives a poetic dimension to the often flat vernacular of the pulps. It is a poet's exuberance to 'run similes into the ground' and from the very start Chandler is able to produce images which reverberate in the mind long after their precise location is forgotten.

It is perhaps this unabashedly literary dimension, plus his passionate pleas to be taken seriously by the critical establishment (which interestingly he found more liberal in England than America) that endears him so much to British crimewriters, though many of us by his own rather strict criteria wouldn't rate much higher then greetings card versifiers!

Not that he reserved his venom for softboiled authors alone. James M. Cain, whose *The Postman Always Rings Twice* is number five on our list, caught it in the neck too. 'Everything he touches smells like a billygoat. He is the kind of writer I detest . . . such people are the offal of literature . . .' Perhaps the essentially romantic Chandler couldn't stomach that the mean streets down which Cain's heroes go lead almost inevitably to destruction. *The Postman* is a fine novel, truly tragic in the Greek sense, with its protagonists in the grip of a passion they cannot control, leading to a crime paid for via the agency of blind chance, not the knight-errantry of some noble PI. Cain is a not unworthy member of this triumvirate which dominates the CWA list. They set a standard and an example which has rarely been matched but which has stimulated writing of a very high level in the decades since.

None of the names that fill the last four places is surprising, though some of the book choices might be. Estleman's Amos Walker amd Parker's Spenser are PI's in the great tradition, yet they belong completely to their own age and give us that unique hardboiled-eye view of two new metropolitan jungles, Detroit and Boston respectively. George V. Higgins does for U.S. low life dialogue what Ivy Compton Burnett did for that of the English upper class. And Elmore Leonard, who probably because of the sheer class of the competition took a long time to get the appreciation he deserves, is marvellously sharp both of ear and tongue. His endings are sometimes a mite too throwaway but it's always great fun getting there, and even if he'd stopped writing *Freaky Deaky* after Chapter One, he'd still have had a prize-winning short story on his hands!

Yet, if the inclusion of these names is not surprising, the omission of others might raise a few eyebrows. Where for instance are the sons of Donald: Ross, John D. and Greg? The first would certainly get many of the critics' votes as the best of the post-Chandlerian era. Where is Jim Thompson, whose nightmarish vision of the underside of the American Dream makes many other hardboilers taste like sunny side up? Why in a list voted for by an association half of whose active members are women does none of the new wave of female hardboilers appear? Where are Sara Paretsky? Sue Grafton? Our own Lisa Cody and Susan Moody? And what of the British men, for the popularity of the style was almost as great over here as over there? Peter Cheyney, whose *Dark Duet* struck Chandler as being 'damn good', is their doyen. James Hadley Chase is another who wrote, if not always convincingly, yet with great pace and panache in the American hardboiled vein. And there are many others such as Mike Ripley and Peter Chambers who keep the Union Jack proudly flying.

But in the end it has to be acknowledged that this is a predominantly American literary form, perhaps the only totally original one. The finest novels it has so far produced are urban poems written by native Americans (all right, so Chandler went to Dulwich, which just goes to show that a good man can survive even an English public school education) with a sharp ear for the speech rhythms of their unique language, a sharp eye for the inequalities and corruptions of their once revolutionary society, and a deep and genuine pain that this is how the Dream has panned out. Far from a slavish realism, it should be recognised that the hardboiled school, like Hollywood with the Western, has created a myth, but myths of course are the best way we have of shaping and controlling chaos. That's what Shelley meant when he said that poets were the unacknowledged legislators of mankind. The alternative is politicians. I rest my case.

Reginald Hill has written twenty novels, his popular detective partnership of Dalziel and Pascoe appearing in ten of them.

SECTION III

The Critics

It was playwright John Osborne who said that asking a working writer what he felt about critics was like asking a lamp-post what it feels about dogs. Nonetheless, we asked four well-known critics what they looked for when they opened a fresh batch of crime novels – or what they hoped not to find . . .

A Local Habitation

MARCEL BERLINS

My geographical insecurity started with Sherlock Holmes.
When I was twelve, I found the stories set in London far
more enjoyable than those in which the great detective
travelled outside. I still do. On graduating to Christie a
year later, I grudgingly accepted the country house as a
proper lieu for the whodunnit, but not – to this day – her
foreign settings, like Mesopotamia or the Nile. No private
eye could have his office anywhere but in Los Angeles,
I decided soon afterwards, and no police department had
any literary right to be outside New York. Over the years,
I extended legitimacy to a few other carefully selected areas;
but my prejudices remained, on the whole, intact. At their
extreme was an aversion to crime novels sited in Aus-
tralia (or, though slightly less passionately, any colony or
Commonwealth country), any sort of open territory (desert,
sea, mountains), any Eastern state, or any English city other
than London.

As a dispassionate critic I have, of course, set aside all such
geographical preferences. I have discovered that wonderful detection can exist in the most unlikely places – Tony
Hillerman's Navajo reservation, for example. But I am
puzzled by one great difference between English and
American crime novels. On the other side, they've managed to find an excellent writer (and accompanying sleuth)
for just about every city on the map: Paretsky's Chicago,
Loren D.Estleman's Detroit and Robert B. Parker's Boston
are justly praised; but there are scores of other excellent
urbanly precise novels, all of them evocatively breathing
the different atmospheres of their settings. But where
are the English equivalents? Where are Newcastle, Bris-
tol, Birmingham, Manchester, Liverpool, and Leeds? Why

have they not attracted their own expert chroniclers? York, through Reginald Hill, has come nearest to being explored in the way that, say, Estleman does Detroit (and in Scotland, Glasgow has attracted a few decent works). It's not just a question of where the action takes place. What the American writers do so well – and the English have not yet accomplished – is to make the city an essential element, a character if you want, of the story. Ten years ago, I would have gone to some trouble to avoid a crime novel set neither in London nor in an English village or sleepy market town. Now I have become obsessed the other way. I await the first great English provincial inner-city whodunnit.

Marcel Berlins reviews crime fiction for The Times *and for the past two years has served as one of the judges for the CWA Gold and Silver Dagger awards.*

Yankee Doodle Doodles

JOHN COLEMAN

As we move into the nefarious Nineties, a fully paid-up admiration for America's criminal authors emboldens me to unleash a few niggles. It is my humble hope that they will provide terrific thesis-fodder for all you budding PhDs out there.

Come snow, come shine, hung over or not, good old V.I. Warshawski wakes up at six in Chicago, puts on her running gear and jogs five miles around Belmont Harbour and back. In Santa Teresa, Kinsey Millhone – another 6 a.m. riser – is doing her three-mile slog along a Californian beach. An even newer accession to the female PI ranks, Linda Barnes's breezy 6'1" redhead Carlotta Carlyle is probably steaming off to the Y in Boston for a brisk game of basketball with her buddies. Always jog, jog, jog! Eh! Ms Paretsky? Ms Grafton? But what you're doing to an otherwise spellbound armchair reviewer is putting his ego (and patience) in a wheelchair, that's what. Don't tell *me* about miles to go before I sleep. No one's memory needs jogging this often.

They do a lot of disconcerting things Stateside, like calling a handbag a purse and nursing republican delusions about our nobs. So it's *ave atque vale* to the Cor-Love-A-Duke school, writers like Martha Grimes and Elizabeth George whose compatriots praise their crime novels as brilliantly set in a contemporary Britain. Well, maybe. Grimes's Hollywood cockneys irately howl for a bobby and a secretary daintily deposits a lipsticked tissue in the dustbin (sic) by her desk: George teams up an inspector-earl, of so wincingly obliging a nobility as to make Wimsey seem a lager-lout, with a lumpen woman sergeant given to chip-on-the-shoulder mopings over her 'weekly pint of ale'. The plots submerge under a gale of giggles.

Another transatlantic puzzler of the wrong sort is the Dressed-To-Kill phenomenon in its masculine manifestation. Over here, we tend to keep pretty tight-lipped about what a fellow or felon sports, with maybe the odd dirty mac or jacket getting a mention. (Holmes was special.) Over there, even Steve Carella's leisure wear ('a plaid mackinaw over a woollen shirt and corduroy trousers') rates attention. A *mackinaw*, yet. When Chandler read the sartorial news, he did it to make a character point. Many other US male crime writers seem to inventory clothes compulsively, like a kid costuming Action Man or as if under contract to Brooks Brothers. By the time one gets to Robert B. Parker's designer-sleuth Spenser, it's narrow pink ties, black Gucci loafers and off-white, straight-legged Levi cords all the way to the next corpse.

But let me loose on Spenser, with his gourmet quotes and grub, his educative/sexy lover Susan, the ethical cop-out of his conscience-saving killer-pal Hawk, and we'll be knee deep in the slither of another can of worms. Next week: 'P. D. James and The Poetry of Adam Dalgliesh'.

EDITOR'S NOTE: Should the worst come to the worst, Mr Coleman asks us to point out that he will be available for proofreading, remedial courses in British English, and the odd children's party (balloon-bursting a speciality).

John Coleman has for many years had a column reviewing crime in The Sunday Times *and has also acted as one of the judges for the Dagger awards.*

De Gustibus

F.E. PARDOE

Deep down I have a conviction that the crime-story is a modern version of the fairy-story, in which all sorts of dreadful things happen but eventually work out so that right triumphs ('They do jest, poison in jest; no offence i' the world').

I'm also conditioned, I suspect, by having come to the crime-story when detectives/heroes were supermen, intellectually at least, and often physically as well.

Having thus clearly established that I am no fit person to be writing about the contemporary crime-story, I propose to stick my neck out even further by stating, with no qualifications, that the best three crime-stories ever written are Conan Doyle's *The Hound of the Baskervilles*, Dorothy Sayers' *The Nine Tailors*, and Michael Innes' *Lament for a Maker*.

As the most recent of those was written over fifty years ago, I feel that I ought to try to re-establish some sort of credibility by saying that I have not read any of the three books for more years than I care to remember. There are too many new books to read – there is no time for re-reading; and in any case I don't want to re-read them: they may well not be as good as I remember them.

But I am also convinced, also without qualifications, that we are at present in the middle of a new Golden Age of crime-writing.

I have never been sure when the original Golden Age took place. The 1920s and the 1930s are usually quoted, but most of the books written before 1930 were mere puzzles, the sort of story epitomised by the Sayers' story built around a crossword puzzle (a very difficult puzzle, as one would expect from her) or by Ellery Queen's habit of stopping his story before the last chapter and challenging the reader to work out the solution to the mystery.

It was not until well into the 1930s that Allingham, Marsh, Innes, Blake and others either started, or developed into rivals of those like Christie, Sayers, Mitchell, who had started in the 1920s.

Now, in this country alone, we have at least half a dozen authors who can easily stand comparison with the writers of the first Golden Age, and there are probably as many more treading closely behind them on the ladder.

I am not going to name names, as I should certainly forget someone for whom I have the highest regard, but, again sticking my neck out, I am prepared to argue that Barbara Vine's *A Fatal Inversion* is the best crime-story written in the last fifty years.

It is all a bit of a nonsense really, this talk of 'the best book' and 'ladders' and arranging books in order of merit. Everybody has a particular idea of what is good, or bad. Certain absolutes exist, obviously, but ultimately it is a question of taste. And there has been no arguing about taste since some Roman, I assume, wrote the original Latin tag.

F.E. Pardoe has headed the Judging Committee for the Gold and Silver Dagger Awards for over twenty-five years. He is also the crime reviewer for The Birmingham Post.

The Ideal Crime Novel

JULIAN SYMONS

1. First of all, it will be conceived as a novel: that is, in terms of the interaction of characters in a form that leads to violence. Does this sound obvious? But it means that the book will *not* be conceived in terms of, say, a tremendously ingenious locked room mystery, or a piece of pure verbal or visual deception of the reader.

2. Which is not to say that cleverness and deliberate deception are ruled out. The point is that they should spring naturally from the natures and motives of the characters. They will be invented first, together with whatever may be the relationships between them leading to crime. The plot should fit the characters: the characters should not be forced into inappropriate actions by a preconceived plot.

3. Everything in the story will relate, directly or obliquely, to the plot. If a red herring or two is trailed before the reader it will prove eventually to be somehow connected with the crime or its consequences. There will be no sub-plots unconnected to the main theme.

4. Yet of course the puzzle element will be, must be, present. Motives may be concealed, words or actions presented in such a way that they are likely to mislead the most attentive reader. Ambiguities may exist, as they do in the question of how fully we can rely on what the governess sees in *The Turn of the Screw*. But again it will be possibilities inherent in the nature of particular human beings that are the cause of bafflement, not something arbitrarily imposed by the author.

5. Should there be a detective, professional or amateur, forensic, ballistic or medico-legal details? These will all be optional, decided by the characters and the crime.

6. The resolution of the story is again to be found in the nature of the people involved and their relationships within the plot. To set things down in this way is inevitably to some extent artificial, as if 'characters' and 'plot' were totally separate. James's masterpiece is an example of the way in which they may be perfectly melded.
7. And the final result of this perfect melding? A novel that wins the Booker.

Julian Symons, himself a well-known crime novelist, has at various times been a critic for most of the national newspapers, most currently for The Independent. *He was recently awarded the CWA's Diamond Dagger for excellence in the genre.*

RONALD KNOX'S DECALOGUE

I THE CRIMINAL must be someone mentioned in the early part of the story, but must not be anyone whose thoughts the reader has been allowed to follow.

II ALL SUPERNATURAL or preternatural agencies are ruled out as a matter of course.

III NOT MORE THAN ONE secret room or passage is allowable.

IV NO HITHERTO UNDISCOVERED poisons may be used, nor any appliance which will need a long scientific explanation at the end.

V NO CHINAMAN must figure in the story.

VI NO ACCIDENT must ever help the detective, nor must he ever have an unaccountable intuition which proves to be right.

VII THE DETECTIVE must not himself commit the crime.

VIII THE DETECTIVE must not light on any clues which are not instantly produced for the inspection of the reader.

IX THE STUPID FRIEND of the detective, the Watson, must not conceal any thoughts which pass through his mind; his intelligence must be slightly, but very slightly, below that of the average reader.

X TWIN BROTHERS, and doubles generally, must not appear unless we have been duly prepared for them.

Reproduced from the preface of Best Detective Stories of 1928–29, *edited by Ronald Knox.*

The Crime Writers' Association

The Crime Writers' Association

Membership is open to published writers of crime fiction and non-fiction. Application for Associate Membership may be made by publishers, agents, producers or reviewers associated with crime stories.

Further details from The Secretary, P.O. Box 172, Tring, Herts HP23 5LP.

A Brief History

The first meeting of the Crime Writers' Association was held on 5th November 1953. The Founder Members were John Creasey (Chairman), Josephine Bell, John Bude, Ernest Dudley, Elizabeth Ferrars, Andrew Garve, Michael Gilbert, Bruce Graeme, Leonard Gribble, T.C.H. Jacobs, Frank King, Nigel Morland, Colin Robertson and Julian Symons.

The following members have been Chairmen of the Association:

John Creasey 1953–7
Bruce Graeme 1957–8
Julian Symons 1958–9
Josephine Bell 1959–60
T.C.H. Jacobs 1960–1
Val Gielgud 1961–2
Charles Franklin 1962–3
John Boland 1963–4
Michael Underwood 1964–5
Philip McCutchan 1965–6

Berkely Mather 1966–7
Gavin Lyall 1967–8
Miles Tripp 1968–9
Herbert Harris 1969–70
H.R.F. Keating 1970–1
John Bingham 1971–2
Christianna Brand 1972–3
Dick Francis 1973–4
Kenneth Benton 1974–5

Jean Bowden 1975–6
Duncan Kyle 1976–7
Elizabeth Ferrars 1977–8
Donald Rumbelow 1978–9
Margaret Yorke 1979–80
Penelope Wallace 1980–1
Basil Copper 1981–2
Laurence Henderson 1982–3

Madelaine Duke 1983–4
Peter Chambers 1984–5
Lady Antonia Fraser 1985–6
Simon Brett 1986–7
Tim Heald 1987–8
Paula Gosling 1988–9
Susan Moody 1989–90
Catherine Aird 1990-91

The Awards

Awards have been presented for the best crime novel of the year since 1955, the original Crossed Red Herrings Award being superseded by the Gold Dagger. The Silver Dagger goes to the runner-up. Since 1978, a Gold Dagger has also been awarded to the year's best non-fiction crime book.

The John Creasey Memorial Award, instituted to commemorate his death in 1973, is for the best crime novel by a previously unpublished writer.

The Diamond Dagger, sponsored by Cartier since 1986, goes to a writer, not a book, and is awarded annually for outstanding contributions to the genre.

From 1986 to 88, *The Police Review* sponsored an award for the crime novel which best portrayed police work and procedure.

In 1988 for one year only *Punch* magazine sponsored a Punch Prize for the funniest crime book of the year. It was thereafter superseded by The Last Laugh Award.

The Award Winners

Titles are out of print unless otherwise stated.

1955

Winston Graham *The Little Walls*, (256 pages, Fontana, £2.50 paperback)
Runners-up: Leigh Howard *Blind Date*
Ngaio Marsh *Scales of Justice* (256 pages, Fontana, £2.99 paperback)
Margot Bennett *The Man Who Didn't Fly*

1956

Edward Grierson *The Second Man*
Runners-up: Sarah Gainham *Time Right Deadly*
Arthur Upfield *Man of Two Tribes*
J.J. Marric *Gideon's Week*

1957

Julian Symons *The Colour of Murder* (256 pages, Papermac, £3.99 paperback)
Runners-up: Ngaio Marsh *Off With His Head*
George Milner *Your Money or Your Life*
Douglas Rutherford *The Long Echo*

1958

Margot Bennet *Someone From the Past*
Runners-up: Margery Allingham *Hide My Eyes* (224 pages, Hogarth Press, £3.95 hardback)
James Byrom *Or Be He Dead*
John Sherwood *Undiplomatic Exit*

1959

Eric Ambler *Passage of Arms* (256 pages, Fontana, £3.50 paperback)
Runners-up: James Mitchell *A Way Back*
Menna Gallie *Strike for a Kingdom*

1960

Gold Dagger: Lionel Davidson *The Night of Wenceslas*
Runners-up: Mary Stewart *My Brother Michael* (254 pages, Coronet, £2.99 paperback)
Julian Symons *Progress of a Crime*

1961

Gold Dagger: Mary Kelly *The Spoilt Kill*
Runners-up: John le Carré *Call for the Dead* (157 pages, Penguin, £2.99 paperback)
Allan Prior *One Away*

1962

Gold Dagger: Joan Fleming *When I Grow Rich*
Runners-up: Eric Ambler *The Light of Day* (224 pages, Fontana, £3.50 paperback)
Colin Watson *Hopjoy Was Here* (158 pages, Methuen, £3.95 paperback)

1963

Gold Dagger: John le Carré *The Spy Who Came in from the Cold* (220 pages, Coronet, £3.50 paperback)
Runners-up: Nicholas Freeling *Gun Before Butter* (224 pages, Penguin, £2.50 paperback)
William Haggard *The High Wire*

1964

Gold Dagger: H.R.F. Keating *The Perfect Murder* (256 pages, Arrow, £2.50 paperback)
Best Foreign: Patricia Highsmith *The Two Faces of January* (284 pages, Penguin, £3.50 paperback)
Runners-up: Gavin Lyall *The Most Dangerous Game* (224 pages, Coronet, £3.50 paperback)
Ross Macdonald *The Chill* (224 pages, Allison & Busby, £3.50 paperback)

Gold Dagger: Ross Macdonald *The Far Side of the Dollar* (256 pages, Allison & Busby, £3.99 paperback)
Best British: Gavin Lyall *Midnight Plus One* (224 pages, Coronet, £3.50 paperback)
Runners-up: Dick Francis *For Kicks* (236 pages, Pan, £3.50 paperback)
Emma Lathen *Accounting for Murder* (186 pages, Penguin, £2.99 paperback)

Gold Dagger: Lionel Davidson *A Long Way to Shiloh*
Best Foreign: John Ball *In the Heat of the Night*
Runner-up: John Bingham *The Double Agent*

Gold Dagger: Emma Lathen *Murder Against the Grain*
Best British: Eric Ambler *Dirty Story* (208 pages, Fontana, £3.50 paperback)
Runner-up: Colin Watson *Lonelyheart 4122* (160 pages, Mandarin, £3.50 paperback)

1968

Gold Dagger: Peter Dickinson *Skin Deep*
Best Foreign: Sebastian Japrisot *The Lady in the Car* (240 pages, No Exit Press, £2.99 paperback)
Runner-up: Nicholas Blake *The Private Wound* (223 pages, Dent, £3.95 paperback)

1969

Gold Dagger: Peter Dickinson *A Pride of Heroes* (156 pages, Arrow, £2.50 paperback)
Silver Dagger: Francis Clifford *Another Way of Dying*
Best Foreign: Rex Stout *The Father Hunter*

1970

Gold Dagger: Joan Fleming *Young Man I Think You're Dying*
Silver Dagger: Anthony Price *The Labyrinth Makers* (239 pages, Grafton, £2.95 paperback)

1971

Gold Dagger: James McClure *The Steam Pig* (223 pages, Coronet, £2.50 paperback)
Silver Dagger: P.D. James *Shroud for a Nightingale* (323 pages, Penguin, £3.99 paperback)

1972

Gold Dagger: Eric Ambler *The Levanter* (272 pages, Fontana, £3.50 paperback)
Silver Dagger: Victoria Canning *The Rainbird Pattern*

1973

Gold Dagger: Robert Littell *The Defection of A.J. Lewinter*
Silver Dagger: Gwendoline Butler *A Coffin for Pandora*
John Creasey Memorial Award: Kyril Bonfiglioli *Don't Point That Thing at Me*

1974

Gold Dagger: Anthony Price *Other Paths to Glory*
Silver Dagger: Francis Clifford *The Grosvenor Square Goodbye*
John Creasey Memorial Award: Roger L. Simon *The Big Fix*

1975

Gold Dagger: Nicholas Meyer *The Seven Per Cent Solution*
Silver Dagger: P.D. James *The Black Tower* (288 pages, Penguin, £3.99 paperback)
John Creasey Memorial Award: Sara George *Acid Drop*

Gold Dagger: Ruth Rendell *A Demon in My View* (184 pages, Arrow, £3.50 paperback)
Silver Dagger: James McClure *Rogue Eagle*
John Creasey Memorial Award: Patrick Alexander *Death of a Thin-Skinned Animal*

1977

Gold Dagger: John le Carré *The Honourable Schoolboy* (602 pages, Coronet, £4.50 paperback)
Silver Dagger: William McIlvanney *Laidlaw* (224 pages, Coronet, £3.50 paperback)
John Creasey Memorial Award: Jonathan Gash *The Judas Pair* (210 pages, Arrow, £2.50 paperback)

1978

Gold Dagger: Lionel Davidson *The Chelsea Murders*
Silver Dagger: Peter Lovesey *Waxwork* (171 pages, Arrow, £2.50 paperback)
John Creasey Memorial Award: Paula Gosling *A Running Duck* (202 pages, Pan, £2.50 paperback)
Non-Fiction Gold Dagger: Audrey Williamson *The Mystery of the Princes* (240 pages, Alan Sutton, £6.95 paperback)
Non-Fiction Silver Dagger: Harry Hawkes *The Capture of the Black Panther*

1979

Gold Dagger: Dick Francis *Whip Hand* (256 pages, Pan, £3.99 paperback)
Silver Dagger: Colin Dexter *Service of All the Dead* (256 pages, Pan, £3.99 paperback)
John Creasey Memorial Award: David Serafin *Saturday of Glory*
Non-Fiction Gold Dagger: Shirley Green *Rachman*
Non-Fiction Silver Dagger: Jon Connell and Douglas Sutherland *Fraud*

1980

Gold Dagger: H.R.F. Keating *The Murder of the Maharajah* (223 pages, Arrow, £2.95 paperback)
Silver Dagger: Ellis Peters *Monk's Hood* (224 pages, Futura, £2.99 paperback)
John Creasey Memorial Award: Liza Cody *Dupe*
Non-Fiction Gold Dagger: Anthony Summers *Kennedy Conspiracy* (657 pages, Sphere, £4.99 paperback)

1981

Gold Dagger: Martin Cruz Smith *Gorky Park* (335 pages, Fontana, £3.99 paperback)
Silver Dagger: Colin Dexter *The Dead of Jericho* (224 pages, Pan, £3.99 paperback)
John Creasey Memorial Award: James Leigh *The Ludi Victor*

Non-Fiction Gold Dagger: Jacobo Timerman *Prisoner Without a Name, Cell Without a Number*

1982

Gold Dagger: Peter Lovesey *The False Inspector Dew* (251 pages, Arrow, £3.50 paperback)
Silver Dagger: S.T. Hayman *Ritual Murder*
John Creasey Memorial Award: Andrew Taylor *Caroline Minuscule* (192 pages, Gollancz, £9.95 hardback)

1983

Gold Dagger: John Hutton *Accidental Crimes*
Silver Dagger: William McIlvanney *The Papers of Tony Veitch* (254 pages, Coronet, £2.99 paperback)
John Creasey Memorial Award: Carol Clemeau *The Ariadne Clue* and Eric Wright *The Night the Gods Smiled* (208 pages, Fontana, £2.95 paperback)
Non-Fiction Gold Dagger: Peter Watson *Double Dealer*

1984

Gold Dagger: B.M. Gill *The Twelfth Juror* (175 pages, Coronet, £2.99 paperback)
Silver Dagger: Ruth Rendell *The Tree of Hands* (269 pages, Arrow, £3.50 paperback)
John Creasey Memorial Award: Elizabeth Ironside *A Very Private Enterprise*

Non-Fiction Gold Dagger: David Yallop *In God's Name* (479 pages, Corgi, £3.99 paperback)

1985

Gold Dagger: Paula Gosling *Monkey Puzzle* (256 pages, Pan, £2.50 paperback)
Silver Dagger: Dorothy Simpson, *Last Seen Alive* (220 pages, Sphere, £3.50 paperback)
John Creasey Memorial Award: Robert Richardson *The Latimer Mercy* (184 pages, Gollancz, £2.99 paperback)
Non-Fiction Gold Dagger: Brian Masters *Killing For Company* (352 pages, Coronet, £4.99 paperback)
Police Review Award: Andrew Arncliffe *After the Holiday*

1986

Diamond Dagger: Eric Ambler
Gold Dagger: Ruth Rendell *Live Flesh* (272 pages, Arrow, £3.50 paperback)
Silver Dagger: P.D. James *A Taste for Death* (513 pages, Penguin, £4.99 paperback)
John Creasey Memorial Award: Neville Steed *Tinplate* (179 pages, Arrow, £2.50 paperback)
Non-Fiction Gold Dagger: John Bryson *Evil Angels*
Police Review Award: Bill Knox *The Crossfire Killings* (218 pages, Arrow, £2.99 paperback)

Diamond Dagger: P.D. James
Gold Dagger: Barbara Vine *A Fatal Inversion* (317 pages, Penguin, £3.50 paperback)
Silver Award: Scott Turow *Presumed Innocent* (423 pages, Penguin, £4.99 paperback)
John Creasey Memorial Award: Denis Kilcommons *Dark Apostle* (336 pages, Corgi, £2.95 paperback)
Non-Fiction Gold Dagger: Bernard Taylor and Stephen Knight *Perfect Murder* (336 pages, Grafton, £3.50 paperback)

Diamond Dagger: John le Carré
Gold Dagger: Michael Dibdin *Ratking* (282 pages, Faber & Faber, £3.50 paperback)
Silver Dagger: Sara Paretsky *Toxic Shock* (320 pages, Penguin, £3.99 paperback)
John Creasey Memorial Award: Janet Neel *Death's Bright Angel* (224 pages, Penguin, £2.99 paperback)
Non-Fiction Gold Dagger: Bernard Wasserstein *The Secret Lives of Trebitsch Lincoln* (416 pages, Penguin, £4.99 paperback)
Punch Prize: Nancy Livingston *Death in a Distant Land* (190 pages, Gollancz, £9.95 hardback)

Diamond Dagger: Dick Francis
Gold Dagger: Colin Dexter *The Wench is Dead* (200 pages, Pan, £3.99 paperback)
Silver Dagger: Desmond Lowden *The Shadow Run* (236 pages, Deutsch, £11.95 hardback)
John Creasey Memorial Award: Annette Roome *A Real Shot in the Arm* (256 pages, Coronet, £3.50 paperback)
Non-Fiction Gold Dagger: Robert Lindsey *A Gathering of Saints* (431 pages, Corgi, £4.99 paperback)
Last Laugh Award: Mike Ripley *Angel Touch* (160 pages, Collins, £10.95 hardback)

Acknowledgements

Many thanks to all those below who filled in the questionnaires and gave us the benefit of their knowledge and enthusiasm.

CONTRIBUTOR:	MOST RECENT BOOK:
R. Adey	*Locked from Murders & Other Impossible Crimes* Ferret Fantasy,
Catherine Aird	*The Body Politic*, Macmillan.
Robert Barnard	*Death & The Chaste Apprentice* Collins Crime Club
Jean Bowden	*Broken Threads* (as Tessa Barclay) W.H. Allen
Simon Brett	*Mrs. Pargeter's Package* Macmillan
Robert Church	*Accidents of Murder* Robert Hale
Liza Cody	*Rift* Collins Crime Club/Fontana
Natasha Cooper	*Festering Lilies* Simon & Schuster
Clare Curzon	*The Blue-eyed Boy* Collins Crime Club/Doubleday
Gregory Dowling	*Neapolitan Reel* Grafton
Marjorie Eccles	*Requiem For A Dove* Collins Crime Club
Martin Edwards	*Executive Survival* Kogan Page
Lorette Foley	*Murder in Burgos* Robert Hale
Anthea Fraser	*Symbols At Your Door* Collins Crime Club
Antonia Fraser	*The Cavalier Case* Bloomsbury
Stephen Gallagher	*Rain* New English Library
Michael Gilbert	*Anything For A Quiet Life* Hodder & Stoughton
Paula Gosling	*Backlash* Macmillan/Pan
Lesley Grant-Adamson	*Curse The Darkness* Faber & Faber
Gerald Hammond	*Let Us Pray* Macmillan

Palma Harcourt	*Double Deceit* Collins
George Harding	
Michael Hartland	*Frontier of Fear* Hodder & Stoughton
Tim Heald	*Business Unusual* Macmillan
Reginald Hill	*Bones And Silence* Collins Crime Club
Miles Huddleston	
H.R.F. Keating	*Inspector Ghote: His Life & Crimes* Hutchinson
Susan Kelly	*Hope Against Hope* Piatkus Books
Alanna Knight	*Deadly Beloved* Macmillan
Isabel Lambot	*Blood Ties* Macmillan
Michael Z. Lewin	*Child Proof* Macmillan
Nancy Livingston	*Mayhem in Parva* Gollancz
Peter Lovesey	*Bertie And The Seven Bodies* Century
Francis Lyall	*The Croaking Of The Raven* Collins Crime Club
Jill McGown	*Murder Movie* Macmillan
Hugh McCutcheon	*The Cargo of Death* Robert Hale
John Kennedy Melling	*The Crime Writers' Handbook* (edit.) CWA & Chivers
James Melville	*The Bogus Buddha* Headline
Gwen Moffat	*Rage* Macmillan
Susan Moody	*Playing With Fire* Macdonald
Margaret Moore	*Dangerous Conceits* Collins Crime Club
Iwan Morelius	*Kriminallitteratur Pa Svenska* 1749–1985
Stephen Murray	*Fetch Out No Shroud* Collins Crime Club
Janet Neel	*Death On Site* Constable
Frederick Nolan	*Alert State Black* Century
Emma Page	*A Violent End* Collins Crime Club
James Pattinson	*Dead Men Rise Up Never* Robert Hale
John Penn	*A Killing To Hide* Collins Crime Club
Stella Phillips	*Dear Brother, Here Departed* Robert Hale
Andrew Puckett	*Terminus* Collins Crime Club
Ian Rankin	*Westwind* Barrie & Jenkins

Julian Rathbone	*The Pandora Option* Heinemann
Robert Richardson	*The Dying of the Light* Gollancz
Mike Ripley	*Angel Hunt* Collins Crime Club
D.W. Smith	*The Fourth Crow* Macmillan
Staynes & Storey	*Grave Responsibility* Barrie & Jenkins
Gene Stratton	*Killing Cousins* Ancestry Inc (USA)
Julian Symons	*Death's Darkest Face* Macmillan
Andrew Taylor	*Blood Relation* Gollancz
Mark Timlin	*Romeo's Tune* Headline
Michael Underwood	*Rosa's Dilemma* Macmillan
John Wainwright	*The Man Who Wasn't There* Macmillan
Barbara Whitehead	*The Girl With Red Suspenders* Constable
David Williams	*Holy Treasure* Macmillan
Hazel Wynn Jones	*Murder in a Manner of Speaking* Collins Crime Club

Special thanks also go to Katie Fulford, Bridget Perez and Peter Spencely for their invaluable help.

Ordering books from The Hatchards Crime Companion

All the books mentioned in **The Hatchards Crime Companion** can be ordered either through your local Hatchards and Claude Gill bookshop, or direct from

The Mail Order Department
Hatchards
187 Piccadilly
London W1V 9DA
(Telephone 071–439 9921,
Fax: 071–494 1313)

How to order

Either write to the above address or telephone 071–439 9921 (24 hours a day) and give details of your order and the address to where the books are to be despatched.

How to pay

Account holders
Simply supply your account number and name with the order.

Cheques
Cheques should be made payable to Hatchards. You may also pay by International Money Order.

Credit Cards
Payment may be made by Visa, Access, JCB and American Express. Please quote your card number and expiry date when you order.

Postage & Packing

Postage and packing is calculated by weight. As a **guide**, please add the following (please note that adjustments may be necessary at the time of dispatch):
UK 20% (minimum £2.75)
Overseas surface 25% (minimum £3.00)
USA and Canada Accelerated Surface Mail 30% (minimum £2.55)
Airmail 85% (please indicate clearly when ordering if Air Mail is required.)

Postage and packing rates may change.